DISCARDED

THE NORDIC TRANSLATION SERIES

Sponsored by the Nordic Cultural Commission

of the governments of

Denmark, Finland, Iceland, Norway, and Sweden

Advisory Committee:

Einar I. Haugen, Harald S. Næss, and

Richard B. Vowles, Chairman

ROSE OF JERICHO

ROSE OF JERICHO

and Other Stories by Tage Aurell

Berättelser

Translated from the Swedish by Martin S. Allwood

In consultation with Tage and Kathrine Aurell

With an Introduction by Eric O. Johannesson

The University of Wisconsin Press

Madison, Milwaukee, London

1968

This translation
published by The University of Wisconsin Press
Madison, Milwaukee, and London
U.S.A.: Box 1379, Madison, Wisconsin 53701
U.K.: 27–29 Whitfield Street, London, W. 1
English translation copyright © 1968 by the
Regents of the University of Wisconsin
Berättelser,
by Tage Aurell, in Swedish,
published by Albert Bonniers Förlag AB,
Stockholm, Sweden
Copyright © 1946, 1949
by Tage Aurell, Stockholm, Sweden
Printed in
the United States of America by
Vail-Ballou Press, Inc., Binghamton, New York
Library of Congress Catalog Card
Number 68-14036

INTRODUCTION

TAGE AURELL, WHOSE STORIES APPEAR HERE FOR THE FIRST time in English, was born in Christiania (now Oslo), Norway, in 1895 but grew up in the Swedish town of Karlstad in the province of Värmland. After completing his education and working some years as a journalist on the staffs of several provincial newspapers, he spent a decade on the continent, in Germany (1920–21) and in France (1921–30). Some of the stimulating impressions he received during those formative years, comprising as they did one of the most exciting, experimental periods in the history of the arts, are reflected in the articles about art and literature which he published in various newspapers and journals both in Sweden and in Norway.

Aurell's first novel, *Tyberg's Tenement* (*Tybergs gård*) appeared in 1932, two years after his return to Värmland (where he has, incidentally, resided since then); it revealed that his long period of apprenticeship had fostered an original theory of fiction. On the surface seemingly but another novel dealing with small town life, *Tyberg's Tenement* did in fact represent something radically new in this genre. Swedish readers and critics, however, who regarded the novels of *tiotalisterna*, the literary generation of the 1910's, as the models for this kind of fiction, were bound to register their disapproval, for most were unprepared to accept advanced experiments in this type of fiction. Contrasted with the breezy prose, the vivid and colorful characters, and the impressionistic descriptions of the milieux that marked the styles of the novelists who had been dominating the Swedish literary scene, *Tyberg's Tenement*, with its restrained and laconic prose, its small format, and its highly objective narrative perspective, resembled a stark woodcut. Like the next two novels, *To and from Högåsen* (*Till och från Högåsen*, 1934) and *Martina* (1937), it brought few laurels to its author, since the readers of the 1930's, busily plowing through the bulky trilogies and tetralogies that constituted the fictional autobiographies of the new novelists of the working class, failed, not surprisingly, to perceive the dramatic intensity underneath the low-keyed and unamplified writing in these pocket-size novels.

The turning point came in 1943 with the publication of a brilliant and sensitive essay by the influential critic Knut Jaensson, in praise of Aurell's novels. In the essay, originally inspired by the reading of Aurell's fourth novel, *Dime Novel* (*Skillingtryck*, 1943), Jaensson maintained that Aurell's novels represented a new development in Swedish fiction. Above all, Jaensson noted that Aurell's novels were the products not of some highly subjective or idiosyncratic vision or temperament but rather of a deliberate and sustained effort to shift the narrative point of view from the omniscient or self-centered author to a tighter, more objective perspective. That this effort was not motivated by the mere desire for experimentation Jaensson recognized as well. He noted that Aurell's basic desire was identical to that underlying all really significant experiments in fiction: to make the reader perceive a new reality, a reality obscured by the older narrative conventions.

Dime Novel may well rank as Aurell's finest achievement in the novel. The action in this story, woven with consummate artistry, is nevertheless very simple and confined within a period of less than two days. The hero, a young barber named Paul Hedenström, newly married and recently the father of a son, is in difficulties. His barbershop is unprofitable, and his wife has left him. The

story communicates his sense of loneliness and despair
and relates his vain efforts to get his wife and son to re-
join him. He dreams of a new start, even of a mutual
suicide pact. All his efforts having met with rebuff, he
finally commits a desperate act: he sets fire to the house in
which his wife is living with her parents, in the vain hope
of winning her back by rescuing her from the fire. Again
his hopes are dashed, for instead of regaining his wife and
son he is, logically yet ironically, arrested and charged
with arson.

This story, told with the utmost economy of means,
with a keen sense for the eloquence of even trivial details,
and without a touch of sentimentality, has, as Knut Jaensson suggested, much of the compelling power which we
associate with the great Russian writers, a Dostoevsky or
a Chekhov. For beneath the unsentimental and ironic
surface, *Dime Novel* expresses a profound compassion for
the fate of human beings whose misery drives them to
such desperate deeds, for the fate of the lonely, the poor,
and the misunderstood. Basically, it is a story of man's
isolation and his vain efforts to establish deep and lasting
contacts with his fellowmen. The presence in the story
of representatives of the Church and of the Law, a minister and a district attorney, who both, significantly, fail
to help or understand Hedenström, does, however, serve
to lend it an added metaphysical dimension. As the lonely
outsider in a hostile and homeless universe, Hedenström
thus joins the ranks of those more familiar Existentialist
heroes, Kafka's K., Camus' Meursault, and Pär Lagerkvist's
Barabbas.

The small format is Aurell's trademark, none of his
novels being much more than one hundred pages in
length. Shorter still are the ten tales which first made
their appearance in two slender volumes, *Shorter Tales*
(*Smärre berättelser*) in 1946 and *New Tales* (*Nya berät-*

telser) in 1949. These tales, of which nine are included in this volume of English translations,* were well received by the critics who had by now read Jaensson's essay, and they undoubtedly constitute Aurell's finest achievements in the art of fiction. Their brevity makes the essential job of re-reading easier, thus exposing more clearly the basic patterns of Aurell's narrative art and the range of his vision.

In reading Aurell, one observes first that he is a regional writer. Like Faulkner, he has created a mythical province that bounds the physical action in his stories. While the town within that province remains unnamed, there are sufficient indications to identify it as Karlstad, Aurell's hometown. Nevertheless, unlike Selma Lagerlöf, his most famous predecessor as a chronicler of the provincial life of Värmland and best known as the author of *The Story of Gösta Berling,* Aurell is not by any means to be labeled a local colorist. Except for some elements of local dialect in the language, no attention is paid in his stories to the picturesque, to the historical past, or to local traditions, customs, lore, or "types." Aurell is aiming at universality: the sparing use of concrete and specific local details does, in effect, transform them into symbols in the human drama he is trying to convey, a drama independent of time or place.

As far as the action is concerned, very little "happens" in Aurell's stories. A man journeys to Stockholm to visit his daughter who has become a prostitute; another has had his hand severed by a saw in the mill; a third meets with a response to his newspaper advertisements seeking a woman companion. A girl goes dancing and contracts the illness that puts an end to her life at the time when she would have wed. Aloneness, illness and death, and sex

* The present volume is based on the 1960 edition of *Berättelser,* which does not include "Assistant Pastor" ("Vice pastor").

are the three major motifs: the universal concerns of man. The characters we encounter are as commonplace as the events. They are mostly simple, ordinary human beings with uncomplicated feelings and needs. Intellectual or ideological questions are rarely debated. Except in "The Assistant Pastor" ("Vice Pastor"), a story not included in this collection, even religion, which often provides an ideological battleground in rural areas, plays little or no role. Of significance is also the fact that the exterior attributes of the characters—physical appearance, dress, personal mannerisms—are almost ignored. Instead the story focuses on a few meaningful details or gestures that reveal the very essence of a person's existence. All this points to the fact that what Aurell is trying to capture above all is some quality of inwardness, some inner reality of the individual. Common to all his characters is also some form of distress—isolation, frustration, illness, the fear of death—the agonies to which all human beings are subject, no matter how insignificant their lives may seem from a social point of view.

The radically new and modern element in Aurell's stories (for modernism is, of course, a way of "making it new") lies, however, in another direction than those already mentioned: it is his bold experimentation with language and narrative point of view. To read Aurell "you must read not only between the lines but between the words as well," as Professor Gösta Holm so aptly suggests in his recent book on the development of Swedish prose, a book in which Aurell is singled out for special attention. The most striking feature of Aurell's language is the break with traditional syntactical patterns. All unnecessary elements have been rigorously weeded out to heighten the emphasis on certain words and sentences, which thus become charged with meaning and import; hence, the incomplete sentences, the frequent absences of the subject, the oddities of punctuation, the many dashes, parentheses, and italics.

The motivations for these bold experiments with language are not difficult to discover. The prime purpose is naturalistic: to conquer new realms for fiction, the realms of the inner life, sensations, feelings, fleeting associations. Within the prose experiments we detect the effort to produce a more authentic form of psychological realism. But a secondary intent is also significant: to involve the reader more actively in the reading experience. The very difficulty of the prose forces the reader to become more attentive, to sharpen his powers of perception; forces him, in effect, to take part in the creative process.

Aurell is often labeled *berättare,* that is, storyteller, a teller of tales, and he does of course name his own narratives *berättelser,* tales. The label "tale" seems rather anomalous in the case of Aurell, however, for the tale should have a storyteller, a narrator, but in his stories the narrator, too, has been eliminated along with many other literary conventions. Isak Dinesen may with justification be called a teller of tales; Aurell may not. Having said this much, one must, however, admit that some of Aurell's stories, and the best of them at that in my opinion, do compel the reader to listen, with a sensitive and attentive ear indeed. In this sense they may be said to fulfill at least one of the basic requirements of the tale: that it have a listener.

There is, of course, a narrator of sorts in Aurell's stories as there is in all stories, but his presence is rarely felt; he is neither the detached narrator who comments, analyzes, and amplifies nor the omnipresent narrator who is the ordering intelligence. Thus even in the stories in which he is recording the inner thoughts of his characters, as in "Rose of Jericho" or "Until the Ringing of the Bell," Aurell refrains from commentary or analysis. His boldest experiments in fiction are, however, those stories in which the narrative is presented not from a single but from a collective point of view: the townspeople, public gossip. Both in "Gatepost" and in "Whitsun Bride" but above all in "The Old Highway" the story is told by means of fragments of the public voice: broken repartees or snatches of conversation overheard, casual opinions voiced on a bus or at the crossroads, proverbs, a refrain from a popular tune or a hymn, a quotation from the Bible. These fragments form a kind of montage to be assembled by the reader, only the montage is not visual but auditory, a montage for voices. Divested of the narrator, of reporting, of descriptive elements, to some extent of characters even, these "pure" stories tend to make narrative art into a form of dramatic art, into a play for disembodied voices.

The aesthetic effects of this original form of narrative art are varied and striking. One effect is what I like to call inwardness: because of the narrator's absence we are allowed to enter more intimately into the consciousness of the characters in the story. Another and perhaps still more significant effect is a sense of immediacy: we are injected into the midst of events without any kind of preparation. Just as in our own lives we cannot find our bearings when we are actively caught up in things as they occur, so in Aurell's stories, lacking a vantage point, we do not know what will happen next. We feel, therefore, that we ourselves are participants in the stories and not mere spectators; like Stendhal's Fabrizio at the Battle of Waterloo, we do not know that it is a great event until we read about it in the newspaper afterward, that is, until at a later date we get some overall perspective on what has transpired. Moreover, because they do not bring events to any definite end, some of Aurell's stories are, in effect, as surprising and as inconclusive as life itself.

The overall vision of life that is revealed in Aurell's

stories is flavored with the irony inherent in human experience. The human beings we encounter and get to know so intimately are mostly trapped in some way. Insignificant though their lives may be, they mirror the general destiny of the majority of mankind: to be caught up in life's ironies. Thus the young girl in "Whitsun Bride" becomes the bride of death and not of life as she had hoped, and the father in "True Confessions," waiting to see the light go on in his daughter's apartment, is taken for a peeping Tom. A disenchanted vision, it is nonetheless deeply imbued with compassion for human suffering.

New Tales seems for the time being to have marked the end of Aurell's career as a storyteller. A novel, *Viktor,* made its appearance in 1955, but it is autobiographical and somewhat different from the earlier works, more conventional in narrative structure. In recent years the storyteller has retired in favor of the essayist, the translator. Aurell's admiration for French culture is beautifully reflected in the collection of intimate travel sketches coauthored by his wife Kathrine and published under the title *Small French Town (Liten fransk stad,* 1954) and in his translation into Swedish of Stendhal's *Le Rouge et le Noir.* From the French he has also translated August Strindberg's *Le Plaidoyer d'un Fou,* better known in English as *A Madman's Defense,* and the same author's *Vivisections.* Among Aurell's other translations are two well-known works from the German, Franz Kafka's *Das Schloss* and Georg Büchner's *Woyzeck.*

It is then above all the early novels and the stories in this volume that constitute Aurell's major achievements in fiction and ensure his place in the history of Swedish literature. Since Aurell is very much our contemporary, it is of course too early to discern what that place will turn out to be. He is obviously a modernist, and, as such, the similarities between his art of fiction and that of his contemporaries, be they Swedish, French, English, or American, are too numerous to be elaborated on. That he has roots in the past, in older narrative traditions, is also obvious. Yet his art is by no means derivative; it is deeply original.

As a regional writer, Aurell seems more akin to the Norwegians than to the Swedes. The proximity of Värmland to the Norwegian border may have some influence on this, and we might also recall that Aurell was born in Norway. The fact remains that he has much of Jonas Lie's respect for the quotidian, Kinck's suggestive power, and Duun's laconism; and, like Tarjei Vesaas, he has brought new and advanced narrative techniques to bear on country life.

Nevertheless, if I were to single out one Scandinavian writer whose works have the most striking resemblance to Aurell's, it would be a Danish and not a Norwegian writer: Herman Bang (1857–1912), also a consummate artist and literary craftsman in the small format and known for such exquisite short novels as *Tine* or *By the Highway* (*Ved Vejen*). Bang, too, concentrated his attention on ordinary people in simple circumstances, on *stille Existenser,* as he called them. Like Aurell, he shied away from moral or ideological arguments, shifting the emphasis onto the universal passions that guide even the humblest human beings. He, too, consciously sought to achieve the objectivity and immediacy of the drama in his novels: avoiding direct commentary or reporting of thoughts and actions, he stressed dialogue and significant gesture, letting the reader assemble the fragments into a unified whole. And like the stories of Aurell, Bang's works reflect an ironic and disenchanted view of life, not without compassion and a sense of humor.

The similarities between Bang and Aurell are too numerous and too striking to be coincidental. That Bang has been one of the masters under whose influence Aurell has come is apparent. Nevertheless, there are some significant differences between the two writers, and it is one of these in particular that stands out as Aurell's original contribution to Scandinavian fiction, namely, his bold experimentation with language, his development of a unique and highly effective prose style. We have already noted some aspects of this style, a style which, it should be added, serves to place Aurell among the masters of modern Swedish prose, together with Vilhelm Ekelund, Pär Lagerkvist, Elmer Diktonius, and Harry Martinson.

The very progressiveness and originality of this prose style is also largely responsible for the general view of Aurell as a "difficult" writer. "Unique," "cryptic," "esoteric," these are some of the epithets commonly applied to his narrative art, and there is little doubt that he is a writer for *the happy few*. However, like the great Swedish aphorist Vilhelm Ekelund, whom he resembles in some ways and of whom he has drawn such a brilliant and intimate portrait in *Roads and Encounters (Vägar och möten)*, his originality has its source not in the mere desire to fabricate new forms of expression but in a sustained and genuine dedication to his craft and in a conscious cultivation of his vision. And, as is true of the aphorisms of Vilhelm Ekelund or of the best works of most modernist writers of significance, the beauty of Aurell's stories lies perhaps in their very difficulty, the benefit and pleasure we derive from them being commensurate with the efforts we, their readers, are willing to make.

Eric O. Johannesson

University of California, Berkeley
August, 1967

BIBLIOGRAPHY

BY TAGE AURELL

Tybergs gård (*Tyberg's Tenement*). Stockholm, 1932.
Till och från Högåsen (*To and from Högåsen*). Stockholm, 1934.
Martina. Stockholm, 1937.
Tre berättelser (*Three Tales*). Stockholm, 1943. (Includes the three works listed above.)
Skillingtryck (*Dime Novel*). Stockholm, 1943.
Smärre berättelser (*Shorter Tales*). Stockholm, 1946.
Nya berättelser (*New Tales*). Stockholm, 1949.
Bilderbok (*Picture Book*). Stockholm, 1950.
Liten fransk stad (*Small French Town*), co-authored by Kathrine Aurell. Stockholm, 1954.
Viktor. Stockholm, 1955.
Vägar och möten (*Roads and Encounters*). Stockholm, 1960.
Skrifter (*Writings*), 4 vols.: I. *Tybergs gård; Viktor.* II. *Till och från Högåsen; Martina.* III. *Skillingtryck; Vice pastor.* IV. *Berättelser.* Stockholm: Bonniers, 1960.

ABOUT TAGE AURELL

Bäckström, Lars. "I Aurells avkrokar." *Klippbok.* Stockholm: Rabén & Sjögren, 1965. Pp. 170–205.
Gustafson, Alrik. *A History of Swedish Literature.* Minneapolis, 1961. Pp. 534–37.
Holm, Gösta. *Epoker och prosastilar.* Stockholm, 1967.
Jaensson, Knut. "Tage Aurell, egenartad berättare," *Bonniers litterära magasin,* 12 (1943), 491–94. Reprinted in *Essayer.* Stockholm, 1946; and in *40-talsförfattare,* ed. Lars-Olof Franzén. Stockholm, 1965.
Karlzén, John. "Hos Tage Aurell," *Svensk litteraturtidskrift,* 10 (1947), 97–103.

Linder, Erik Hjalmar. *Fem decennier av nittonhundratalet,* II. Stockholm, 1966. Pp. 636–39.

Nerman, Bengt. "Gobeläng med lyssnare," *Bonniers litterära magasin,* 22 (1953), 581–88.

Tykesson, Elisabeth. "Tage Aurell, författare," *Svensk litteraturtidskrift,* 8 (1945), 183–90. Reprinted in *Tolv essayer.* Stockholm, 1945.

CONTENTS

UNTIL THE RINGING
OF THE BELL

THEY'VE SEEN IT DOWN AT THE POST OFFICE.

Emil Flodman (who's filling in for the country mail-man till the first of August) has seen it.

So has the old devil here at home.

From the tin mailbox over at the bend all the way here.

Then he puts the letter back on the chair where it was lying and takes the newspaper with him to the table, but not the letter.

Now Elin comes rattling in through the door and, pant-ing, puts the two water buckets down right on the thresh-old; she can't make it any farther because of her pain. When she sees that the letter is still lying there, her pant-ing turns into a sigh—she had gone out to get the water as soon as she heard Enok start down the attic stairs.

And figured that by now he would have picked up the letter.

She feels in a quandary—she often does now since she found out that she's ill.

Enok rivets his eyes on the newspaper but sees nothing except the letter. A disgusting letter; where the ring had been, there is now a hole right through the paper and the envelope.

Elin has reached the stove and must rest a while once more. There are two other chairs, yet she returns to the chair by the door. She takes the letter between her fingers (he might guess how gingerly between her fingers) and moves it over to the blanket on the bed.

At last she speaks a few words.

"I moved it," she says.

And then:

"How can anybody get this tired."

The first is like an apology for moving the letter; the second changes abruptly into harshness—he's not the only one that's got pain.

She wants room for hers!

He tries to shift the wad of bandages wound around what used to be his right hand—again pretending to see something worth reading in the paper. But all he sees is how helpless the wad looks as it slides without any grip over the oilcloth.

She sees it too.

Maybe his pain is worse.

"No!" she says out loud.

And pressing her arms across her stomach with the pain darting from her eyes, she looks straight at the letter; only men give in to pain. And even if the pain of his hand is worse, there's no reason for him to take on so about that engagement ring. She, for one, is going to bake now and she needs the blanket for the bread to rise on.

The letter goes from the bed over to him.

To the edge of the table.

To the very edge of the table.

And it can just as well stay there, he is thinking.

He won't touch it anymore.

He realizes too late that that was a stupid idea. For now the old devil stands there ogling the letter—rocking forward and backward in his canvas shoes, lips pursing and tongue waggling from cheek to cheek.

Just like he always does when a choice sneer lies in the offing.

"Maybe she cut it out herself? What do you think?"

Actually, it doesn't really sound sneering, more like a

kind of taking sides. Against women and their ways—
father and son in alliance—

Oh no, no alliance!

"She probably went and sold the goddamn ring. You
might as well have bought a cheaper one."

The many carats in the finger gold were just what
they'd flashed around on Easter Eve. And Enok had said
straight out that sometimes even in this house things
happened like they ought to—his father had just started
in on his whore-chasing up on the ridge then and sat there
looking guilty. Flashed around an engagement party and
twenty-four carats in front of him.

"How about letting me borrow the ring you've still got?
Hunh? Just till the next time. . . ."

And then in outright scorn:

"Whenever that may be. . . ."

The table scrapes across the floor toward the bed, the
geranium pot wobbles, and the chair falls over as Enok
jumps up. Except now the old devil is no longer within
arm's length but is almost at the door. And before he can
get over there, Elin hangs onto him; he beats at the air
above her head, while her apron and skirts twist and
twine around his legs. Of course, he is strong, and if he
were only near the door where that old devil is pushing
down the doorhandle, his left fist could do the job. In a
frenzy his five fingers claw the air, his nails tear at the
empty air.

Elin, on the other hand, is not strong; she can't head
him off any longer. Yet those two must not fight; the
chapel bell may be ringing soon. They shall not fight un-
less it's over her dead body! She gets a better grip around
Enok's waist. She remembers suddenly how they tripped
each other in the schoolyard; both of them topple heavily
to the ground. This one second, for a few seconds, it's like
playing a guilty game, like in the hayloft—from over there

by the door comes a clucking sound; their father sees what their reeling over looks like.

Then he can see that it's going to be harder for them to get up than down; first Elin must get out of the way or Enok will trample on her stomach, the way she's lying. And she has hold of his left hand and Enok can't push himself up on the wad of bandages.

The old man had not been really scared at any time. And as ugly as it now looks, it's not funny anymore—he pushes the door open and is about to walk out.

"We shouldn't be fighting, should we?" he says.

Out on the porch, he says it again through the open door, shaking off Enok's troubles as it were, yet keeping the right and proper amount of compassion.

"*We* shouldn't be fighting."

Greater compassion and, better still, togetherness—those are Elin's feelings as she wriggles out from under the heavy body, gently maneuvers the wad of bandages, and tries with all her might to help him up.

But Enok's whole wrath turns on her for getting in his way.

"Thanks a lot for your help!" he jeers. And he begins to seethe with the same suspicions the old devil had.

"You ought to flop over with someone else! Before it's too late."

He does not feel sorry about what he is saying, since, as he sees it from here, her back is cold and unfeeling.

A moment later he can hear she's crying.

Then he feels like a kind of animal—and he also knows that, among all the bitter moments since his fingers flew up to the sawmill ceiling, the memory of this moment will remain too. Elin has always been the kindest one to him. And if it's really true that this thing with her stomach is dangerous—again she presses her arms to her belly;

when she has got herself down into a chair, the pain
glances from her eyes again.

He grabs the letter and bolts up the attic stairs.

RIGHT AT THE BEGINNING THERE IS A HOLE AND WORDS MISS-
ing where the ring was cut out. From what he can decipher,
things aren't now the way they were when she came
to the hospital during the visiting hour. "You may never
believe it," he reads. "But please understand, Enok. It's
not so easy for me either. Maybe it's harder for me"
(Elin's thought, as different as they may be otherwise).
"You know there are artificial hands that are almost as
good as real hands. You can move them at the wrist."
Here she's turned the paper, and again the hole is there,
but he gathers from the words on both sides of the hole
that it has to do with the price of such hands. "But what
in heaven's name am I to do with myself? He is married.
He wants me to keep the engagement ring, but I can't do
that. Enok. I couldn't do that to you, so I am returning it
to you here. I have kissed the date inside it farewell. He
has three children; the youngest is just two. Awfully cute.
But I'm crying at night." Another hole. Half a hole.

"I don't give a damn about your crying!" Enok tells the
letter, tells his loneliness.

"The other woman doesn't know anything; we just
exist here together. You can guess how this must be for
me. Why did things have to turn out this way? How long
did the narcissuses stay fresh in the hospital? I bought two
for myself, too. I didn't throw them away but cut them
off, and now I have pressed them in my health insurance

book. My pay is pretty good here so I'm not complaining.
But still it seems wrong to take it; that's how I feel sometimes at night. Then I get mad at myself and that's good
because then I don't cry. He earns quite a lot. He too is
in the lumber business. Oh, dear, now I'm crying again.
Can you believe it—he gives his own wife an allowance,
two hundred-crown notes the other day, but she just sat
there holding onto them and looking funny while I was
clearing the table. Now I'll have to end this sad letter of
mine. I've been looking for the jeweler's box but can't
find it. Your former Eyvor." But no, she doesn't end there
at all, not she. "P.S. Please think seriously about getting
one of those artificial hands, and if you'll accept some of
my pay, I could send it by postal money order. P.P.S. It's
awful it had to happen like that at the sawmill. But dear,
dear Enok, don't think it's just because of that. We could
always have found some way."

HUNH, AS THE OLD DEVIL WOULD HAVE SAID. FOUND SOME
way—sure. That's what he had been saving for, an artificial hand! Anyway, he's going to get more money, from
the lumber company; they didn't have the required safety
guard for the blade. He's got a lawyer, too, and he's going
to appear in court next month.

"So you see, an engagement ring more or less, my dear
former Eyvor! That's just so much crap to Enok now; you
damn well don't have to worry about me anymore," he
says out loud in his loneliness.

Could she really have cut the ring out herself? No,
that's just one of the old devil's ideas; only he could
dream up something like that. But she'll get paid for the

narcissuses; she'll get a money order. And here is the jeweler's box; he'll put her ring in it and send it by registered mail so the blasted lumber business will see—

He looks down at the letter again.

Bryggaregatan 12, that's the address.

Who cut out the ring? Maybe the city mail carrier? There she is, walking along one evening, and slips the letter into the mailbox. Later on, up swoops a young nut on a yellow bicycle, unlocks the lid, grabs a handful of letters, and stuffs them into his sack.

At the bank? But Bryggaregatan doesn't pass by the bank; he once stood there at the iron bars a long time; his money is in there. Deposits it at the office down here, but of course it goes into the city, in behind the bars where he had kind of kept guard off and on for an hour in the early hours of the morning that time when he'd missed the train.

How can he get that damned ring off his finger? He had put on weight at the hospital.

He scrapes it against the edge of the table; that wad of bandages doesn't help him any. He can get the ring as far as his knuckle, and there it stops. He tries to use one of the vest buttons to pry it off. He's wearing a vest now; he wears his Sunday best every day now.

Puts the wad of bandages over it and pinches it down. But that never works.

Then he tries to get the ring between his teeth, tries to get a firm bite on it. The tips of his fingers slip down his throat and he almost vomits. He goes to get his shaving mirror to help him see what he's doing, but instead he sees only his eyes bugging out. He raises the back of his hand up against his mouth and tries to press his ring finger against his front teeth.

It sends chills all the way up to the roots of his hair.

At last he just sits there kind of jabbing at the ring,

feebly jabbing at it. There is sweat on his brow and his eyes are glassy from his useless effort, and his cheeks are white-streaked from his nearly throwing up.

Go to the smith to have it cut off? Stand there with his left hand stretched out? Certainly, there wouldn't be any nasty cracks, not at the smith's; he never talked about what happened to people, wouldn't so much as raise an eyebrow even if he were told that the blade had taken the head as well as the fist. But other comments would follow, sure as doomsday, a hell of a long and dry harangue about Judge Rutherford who understood everything so much better than any mother's soul on earth. And from Rutherford he would gradually come to the conclusion that neither the blade nor women nor a ring was of any importance whatsoever.

Enok is pushing and pushing feebly with his thumbnail.

But with soap? He tries to figure how he would go about it. How he could soap his finger all around the ring without being able to use his right hand. Then sits listening to Elin working down there in the kitchen. When might she have an errand outdoors so he can be alone with the soap? She's piling fuel on the fire now for baking, and then he hears that there aren't many sticks left in the bin. That means she'll soon have to go to the woodshed. And that takes her quite a while nowadays; he's noticed how she stops to catch her breath between every other piece of wood.

Maybe she's the worse off of the two of them after all—

There she went out! And like an animal afraid of being discovered, he steals down the attic stairway.

He himself notices his stealthy steps, the haste he makes, like a thief.

"A thief," he says out loud.

SO THAT'S WHAT IT CAME TO, HE'S STILL THINKING AS HE shuffles around the kitchen—goddamn saw, goddamn ring!

For one thing he has put on a lot of weight from sitting quiet so much, and for another he is cursing more than he ever used to.

From keeping quiet so much.

But supposing it was she who cut it out after all? Maybe the old devil and she understand each other, kind of know what to think of one another. That you should never think good of anyone—and she probably thought: He really doesn't need a ring now. He has saved a pretty penny at the bank, and he'll get more from the company, so I'll take it back to the jeweler. On my way home I'll go into the store and buy some silk panties that'll put some pep into the lumber business; that fellow has two good hands for finding out about things like that. The other woman can sit there and stare at her hundred-crown notes—

But now he has been making up stories too long, and he hasn't got hold of a bit of soap yet before Elin is back with the wood carrier. Probably been hurrying, thought she mustn't stay away too long at a time; my goodness, something might happen here and then she ought to be right at hand; crazy menfolk shouldn't be left alone for too long.

No one ever remembers that *she* has such pain she could cry out loud, that *she* could use a little consideration. Besides it might just take Enok's mind off himself to go and get some wood; he needs only one hand to pick up the pieces and no more than one arm to carry a full wood carrier.

While ten or twelve small sticks are a load, more than a load, for her now—

"Help me get this goddamn thing off!"

He holds out his hand to her, five fingers stiffly outspread, the only five fingers he's got left.

"I said, help me!"

There is a lump in his throat—like on the way to the hospital, like one of the times she came to see him, like when he came home.

Which hadn't happened to him since that first time he came to blows at the dancing pavilion in the forest when his confirmation jacket was torn.

And with a great sob he takes the box from his pocket; with a great sob he opens it.

It's just like a little bed.

But then he bites back the tears and wipes the wad of bandages over his eyes. She doesn't approve of that last act; she wants the wad to be nice and white for Sunday. Like a new mat of spruce twigs out on the porch step, like the shirts freshly ironed for him and the old devil, she wants the bandage also to look Saturday-clean and nice. She has even felt in more of a Sunday mood on those Saturdays when he's returned from the hospital with a fresh bandage.

They get it off with soft soap and her help; she has twisted and turned the ring until her forehead is damp with sweat. As for him, both his hands are aching—his left hand aches just as much as what's inside the wad of bandages. But anyway, there it lies, the ring! And in the air there lingers something like a faint echo from a moment ago when it finally rolled down onto the drop-front of the cupboard.

He won't touch it! And yet it is only a few months, a few weeks, since he'd kept turning it round and round, looking at his image in it every time he had washed his hands.—*But it belongs to him!* He paid for both the rings; he might as well keep it, hide it somewhere, keep it as proof that once he too had been engaged, take it out to look at it in his solitude, never send it back—or do like she did, like the old devil said she did, put it in a letter and then cut it out again; he could be that sly too—

But just how would that be done? Should he stand there watching Elin do it for him?

No! The whore of the lumber business will get it back! Then she can get money for it; poor girl, maybe things aren't so easy for her, just like she writes—She'll get it in a small parcel, registered so it'll be sure to reach her; Elin can handle that, take it to the post office when she goes to the bazaar tonight. He'll give her his entrance fee; that'll be his big summer party! She can enter by the back door; of course they'll accept this parcel even if it won't go till Monday—she'll have to register the parcel. Contains one ring, she'll write; of course they'll accept it. Then they'll have something to talk about on their way to the bazaar, something to talk about tomorrow during all of God's long Sunday.

And on Tuesday maybe Eyvor will cry a little—

"Why don't you come along to the bazaar too," says Elin. "Just for a little while."

He won't be going to the bazaar, no, not tonight and not ever. When they are all through with this picky little job of theirs, he'll return to his room in the attic; he'll sit there like an owl, just staring. He'll have his bowl of food put on the stairway; he'll kind of wall himself in; nothing in the whole world will ever bother him anymore—year in and year out—

BUT SHE FORGOT ABOUT THE BOWL. AND WHEN ENOK AIMS to go to the pantry to get something to eat, there is the old devil shaving. And might it be because he has a straight razor in his hand that he's looking so brave, beaming forth his advantage? An advantage when it comes to women, an advantage which doesn't give a damn about rings and all such stuff. For instance, that newfangled idea here at Easter—just what came of that? No point, no point at all in taking women so seriously that you start dreaming by a circular saw and have your fingers fly up to the ceiling.

New shirt. Saturday night. And sporting over the ridge instead.

He strops the razor once more; she must feel as little as possible of his pig's hide.

Feel it as smooth as he can possibly make it!

And of course he'd prefer to live in peace with his miserable boy too—but he doesn't know how to begin that peace; he repeats the words spoken at the door a while ago:

"*We* shouldn't be fighting, should we. . . ."

He is not altogether comfortable; when he's through shaving, it takes him a good long time to clean the razor. As an excuse for keeping it in his hand, he starts in on his malformed toenails, forgets that the old razor is for that—for now he wants Enok to join him in merrier thoughts, wants a bit of fun for him too so he won't just be wandering around here staring at the wad of bandages—he tells him about some sheets of music which Emil Flodman's father had sent for and which they are planning to scrape away on tomorrow afternoon.

"First the damned thing is in major

"tradi ri
"tradi ri
"tradi radi ralla."

He swings the old razor, the one he uses for his toenails,
now he's remembered it, like a conductor's baton—
"But then, goddammit, it trails off into minor

        "hadi
        "hadi
        "rullan lei. . . ."

LOOK AT HIS FATHER SCURRYING ALONG. MAJOR. TRADI RI,
tradi ri, tradi radi ralla.

Here it's minor. Hadi, hadi, rullan—

With his left hand he nips the cork out of the inkwell
and dips his pen. First he practices an E, En, Enok.

Uglier and uglier, sloppier and sloppier it looks to him.
He dips the pen again. E, Ey, Eyvor, that's not any too el-
egant either. Then he makes a sketch, a sort of vengeful
sketch; that comes easier. He is warming up; he presses
down hard. And then the rusty old nib breaks right off.
Immediately he hurls the penholder out the open window—but his fury subsides again almost as fast as it came;
he sees how awkwardly his left arm did the throwing, how
the wad was helping too. How it heaved itself out into
the air, willing but powerless. Now the chapel bell is ringing, the bell that arrived when he lay in the hospital. A
childish, stupid little ringing, he thinks, as he'd thought
the first time. He'd expected more of a sound than that.

TRUE CONFESSIONS

JOHAN TJÄDER IS GOING ON A TRIP NOW.

Because they are getting more and more insistent, he claims.

Letter after letter about the same thing.

But then he figures that if he really does get time off from the power plant to go to the city, he wants to feel footloose and free for once. He wants to get himself a room in a hotel.

And Blomkvist at the co-op store thinks this is a great idea, and to pass over that business about the letters as quickly as possible—there have not been many of them—he reaches for his pencil and an old envelope and begins to draw a map.

"Now, look at this, Johan. Now, first of all you see the Central Station here."

But then he quickly skips over to the hotel, both because of Tjäders' fib about the letters and because of his own ever-vivid recollections of the pleasures he enjoyed at the convention. They called it a temperance hotel but they had been given absolutely everything a man could ask for. In room number twenty-seven, he draws a two and a seven over the whole blank route from the Central Station.

"And that gal who brought the bottles. . . ."

Now Blomkvist is scribbling around the number—an intent and somewhat embarrassed doodle—Johan Tjäder's younger girl worked at a hotel for a while. Blomkvist blurts out, "She was dark-haired and real frisky. . . .

"And she wasn't expensive either."

At that point he finally checks himself; with black

strokes he scratches out both the number and the doodle and then his special memories, moves on from the hotel out into the teeming crowds.

"All in all, it was a real nice convention," he says.

But Johan Tjäder doesn't hold much with that discretion business; on the contrary, he answers brazenly that this is just about what he had in mind. If he really gets time off to go, that is.

And sure enough, the train is rattling and puffing along. Now and then there is quite a festive air about this day; at one or two stations he even gets out to buy himself a soft drink.

He tells his traveling companion in the window seat opposite his about his daughter in Stockholm, one of his daughters. That she was given the name of Johanna once upon a time because his name is Johan. That she is married and has children. He tells about his grandchildren at length, and he can hear that this sounds quite right and natural.

His acquaintance is not going all the way, not by any means. And when they have said goodbye, he feels lonely although all the seats are taken.

Later on in the day, toward dusk and as night falls, he finds just opposite him a girl who looks something like Elsa. At last he barely glances stealthily in her direction; between times he turns his face toward the window.

It is raining now, and black soot trickles down the glass. The train clatters over a bridge, over dark water. And "Go back home!" he'd like to say to the girl opposite. "Go the other way."

All around them the chatter is about streets, about the people who are supposed to be meeting someone at the station; they are primping up, pulling and tugging at bags and suitcases. As for himself, he takes out his ticket and looks carefully at the words "Round Trip," steels himself with them as more and more lights flash by, yellow, red, green. For otherwise this would be a doubtful thing, difficult and doubtful.

He sits for a long time on the side of his bed, doesn't take off his clothes, just the new shoes that have been pinching him for more than ten hours.
Every so often he walks softly over to the window, to the door, then back to the bed. Twiddles one of the brass knobs for a while.
Of course, this is a religious hotel, with a Bible and a hymnbook. But he contents himself with reading the ads on the sides of the blotter and the letters on the cover of the phone book.
Blomkvist's women.
In his wallet there is a faded old class picture which her school mistress once took.
If only they would never grow up.

THE ONLY ADDRESS HE HAS IS THE ADDRESS OF HIS OLDER daughter; he asks the way there, street by street. But he didn't come here for that. Johanna and he were far apart even when she was still at home; she had kept to her mother and the Bethel chapel.
Now supposing Elsa is on vacation—as he walks along, he gives her an orderly existence, a job with vacation.
The stores are opening now; he slips into the first bakery he sees and buys candy and cookies.

"Goodness, is it you?"
Her voice has never been exactly cordial, not to him at any rate, and of course she doesn't like to be taken by sur-

prise in a kitchen which is messy and still uncleaned for the morning.

"You might have written before you came. . . . But sit down, by all means."

Her husband has gone to work, and with the candy the two boys also disappear. On a sofabed sleeps a little girl whom he hasn't seen before. He makes a fuss over her and wonders whom she favors—and all of a sudden he gets a strange desire to say that she looks like Elsa. Then he would soon draw out what he especially wants to know something about.

But there is no likeness. And not enough courage in his chest.

Johanna goes to the pantry with the cookie bag without opening it and in its place brings back a few rusks and biscuits in a bowl, wipes off a corner of the kitchen table, and puts a cup and saucer there.

Then she grinds the coffee for a long while before she asks:

"You aren't going to the hospital, are you?"

Abruptly and suspiciously she blurts out the next question hard on the heels of the first:

"Or has she been writing? Is that it?"

He still hesitates to ask his own questions; instead he says that letters are none too frequent from either one of them, so he just wanted to visit a little.

The realization that he would need somewhere to stay flickers in her eyes; he can see that. So he tells her about the hotel. And that he plans to go back home just as quickly as he came, probably day after tomorrow.

There is an expression of relief around her mouth but she has enough sense to say:

"So soon?"

Neither this kitchen nor the reception nor she herself is as it ought to be—nothing is as it ought to be and least of all the object of his easily-read thoughts:

"You'd better go there in the daytime. Wouldn't be worth your while later."

Now he knows. And can hear both her smugness and her cruelty—both hears them and doesn't hear them—as she continues quite unnecessarily:

"Yes, she has plenty of time during the days. Not like it is for someone who has to keep on toiling and drudging forever."

A moment later she pushes aside the comparison, even the possibility of a comparison:

"I would be ashamed; I would. . . ."

This time he is just as quick as she is:

"We won't talk anymore about Elsa," he says. "Just let me have her address."

"I don't have it," she answers.

He can see that she is lying. And she corrects herself:

"Because maybe she isn't living there anymore. She keeps moving all the time."

"You don't have to go along," he answers to this last comment. "I'll find it okay. I found my way here from the hotel all right. You just write it clearly."

"Go along? Me? Why, you don't. . . ."

But she isn't defending herself as hard as before; she explains exactly how he should go. And doesn't lay claim to his time, not today.

"After that you'll probably want to go back to the hotel to rest up, I suppose."

THE VERY THINGS HE DIDN'T WANT TO SAY DO SLIP OUT. Like this he's saying now:

"What are you doing tonight?"

Timidly and promptly he changes it:

"But I'm sitting here with you right now, aren't I? So if I come back for a little while tomorrow . . ."

Even more promptly:

". . . then I think you'll have seen enough of me."

When she doesn't ask a single question, doesn't protest:

"I can never stay away from home very long, as you know."

Know?—she knows and he knows that this doesn't jibe. For instance, no one's waiting for him at the hotel; he just clings to Johanna's schedule, as it is.

"In a little while I'll be toddling off. I'm going to lie down and take a rest."

Coming all this long way to tell her that he's going to lie down to rest, the big, strong fellow that he is, jibes even less.

She doesn't help him any, neither with truth nor with lie, not even like Johanna's "So soon?"

She was in bed when he came a while ago. Asked angrily through the door who the hell it was that—

He couldn't bring himself to answer; when she opened the door, he was just standing there quite still:

"Oh, Daddy. . . ."

A little frightened but a little happy too.

He already suspects that this may be his only gain from the trip.

At first her face was white. But when she had dressed behind a screen, she came out fresh and rosy. And cocky like in the old days, like her last evening home:

"Now then, why are you comig to see me? Why can't you leave me alone? I'm not a child anymore. You're biting your tongue, of course, but I know what you're asking even though you aren't saying anything. Don't you think I don't understand why you've come. It's that noble Johanna who got you here. To have a look at me! Well, why don't you look? Look! Look! So you'll be satisfied at last! I like it here, do you hear that? I like it here."

He heard it. Heard all of it. And he thinks, if only she'd ask for the address of the hotel now. And as if to make certain—because he isn't quite sure how well he's going to bear up this evening in case he doesn't get to meet with her here—he describes this address of his thoroughly and carefully. Until he completely grasps that he is going to be alone anyhow.

He quickly brushes it aside, the same as he did with Blomkvist—that hotels are great so he can be footloose and free.

And now he is sitting here; it's right here and now he must defend her against all the others, side with her against them. And he must find something they can talk about, restfully and childishly, so *she* can be a child again for a little while; that's really the only way they know each other. Just so everything will be nice and comfortable.

"Say, that's fine furniture you've got."

Neither her mouth nor her eyes are childish; they are full of scorn.

"Oh, yeah. Is that what you think? You really know a lot about it, don't you?"

And then full of hate she rants on:

"Making fun of me, are you?"

Her eyes fill with tears, tears of anger. She tilts the easy chair she's standing behind and lets it down with a heavy thud.

"Goddamn drivel," she says.

But right after that she isn't up to it either, isn't up to the whole truth, to any truth at all.

"He's away on business right now. But I want you to meet him the next time you come to Stockholm. He's a salesman for an awfully big company. Real solid, let me tell you. His ma lives in Småland and we're going there when he gets back. And we're going to get engaged and for a present he's going to give me a fur coat, a muskrat."

Then she cuts herself short again:

"Don't you believe me?"

She goes to the mirror, shakes her black hair, looks at the watch on her wrist.

"So you're going to the hotel," she says over her shoulder. "Well, I'd better get a move on too. I work half a day at a laundry. Rather tiring sometimes."

Laundry on the moon and mother-in-law in Småland, where does she dig all that up from? It's pitiful, yet in the midst of it all he feels a kind of pride and a kind of renewed mutual understanding.

Since he doesn't want just to pull out his wallet, he tries a roundabout way:

"It's your birthday pretty soon, isn't it?"

And then he awkwardly pushes the biggest bill under an ashtray. One corner is visible; that it's a big bill is evident.

But nothing is said about their meeting tonight. And not a word about the following day.

HE HAS A FEELING THAT HE MAY HAVE WALKED TOO FAR ALready and lost his way. But as he turns around now, there is a light shining in a window right across the street, and all of a sudden he's quite sure it's her window. The only lighted window in a big dark wall. And besides, there is a railroad loading dock or something like that over there at the end of the street. And long, silent rows of freight cars.

Still farther off a locomotive is puffing, stopping, and whistling.

Then someone comes up to the window; he can't see if it's she herself or someone she's with. Things are swimming before his eyes, like last night at the hotel. Immediately the window is empty again except for the light, then quite black like the other windows.

Then he decides that he won't go right away; now he'll stay here and wait.

But the window soon lights up again, brighter than before, as if from two lamps instead of one. He strolls over to the loading dock, doesn't look around but straight out into the darkness above the freight cars and the tracks.

Maybe it'll be switched off when I turn around again, he is thinking. Then I can go and stand where I was standing.

Only a weaker light. And he is about to move on once more when suddenly he has company at his side in the dark—a brakeman or something; a patent leather strap and a button shine in the drizzle.

He doesn't know how he'll be able to say to this other one:

"Go home and go to bed. Don't stand around here ogling."

"Is she naked?" asks the brakeman.

First he feels as if he were paralyzed from his head down to his feet. And yet he can hear that the other one doesn't sound fresh, just lonely and also kind of grateful.

"I saw her naked once. Last fall. Since then I usually stop here and wait for a while. Whenever I get off from work at this time."

Then there is silence for several dragging minutes.

"D'you know her?"

The brakeman gets no distinct answer, but he gathers it's no.

"Me neither," he says. "But I know where she hangs out. Boy, is she ever a gorgeous piece."

HE PAID FOR HIS ROOM LAST NIGHT AND GOT A RECEIPTED bill. And he did tip much more than he needed to—there was no more merrymaking this time—he wakes up with the same thought he had just before going off to sleep— that this way he's left behind a good reputation if they should ever hold another convention here. After that he recalls another thought from last night: that maybe I'll be robbed during the night since I showed I've got plenty of money.

Both his purse and his wallet are still under the pillow. And his watch is there, five of three.

He's all set many times over before four o'clock but gathers from the stillness that no street doors are open yet. Like another Blomkvist he sits enthroned at the desk, with the telephone and the penholder. He has a feeling that just this is going to be a big part of his trip story once he's back home again—what he could cope with at a hotel.

Steps sound in the empty street, a faucet gushes, a door slams. The new day begins.

Then he picks up his suitcase and goes to Johanna; there's nothing more for him to wait for here.

Johanna goes with him down to the Central Station; his son-in-law settled that. Also stopped her short when Johanna began her laments about Elsa's way of life.

"Shut up, Johanna. And let your father go in peace."

They are there in plenty of time; he buys apples and licorice and chocolates for the youngsters and an orange for the baby girl on her arm. Then Johanna stands with him for a quarter of an hour or so in the line; she's still holding both the baby and the candy bag with the same arm and so she has a hand free for another ten-crown note to be put into.

She thanks him but doesn't look at him, not even when they are on the platform, by the train steps. Then she's staring far off, toward the engine.

"There's not much time now," she finally says, turning with a jerk. "You'd better get onto the train. Say goodbye to Grandpa, June."

He is holding a thin little hand in his. And Johanna takes her eyes off the locomotive and says with as much cordiality as she is capable of:

"Next time plan to stay longer. And write so I can have things in order when you come."

Now, look at that. Now look, here comes Johan Tjäder. Off the very back of the freight train; now he's standing about fifty meters from the station.

I can take a short cut across the tracks, he's thinking, and over the fir hedge.

But the highway is not quite empty; he can see that he'll have the most privacy skirting the depot. Besides, the ticket is in his hand.

"You didn't stay very long," says Pettersson, the shunter. "Let's see, when did you leave? On Monday?"

"At any rate it was longer than I had figured," is his answer.

And then he adds:

"The main thing is to get together now and then."

He flops down on a bench to rest and stares at the shunting. And he knows what to say anyway; he had thought of trying out his line on Pettersson, but then he couldn't be bothered. He has taken a good look at things, and his story is just as good as Blomkvist's. They didn't stay put at the hotel; they hopped around from one restaurant to another—he had stood for quite a while outside one where there were flowers in boxes and everything just as showy as the finest garden. And the menu framed behind glass.

He and Elsa most of the time.

Johanna not so often because of the kids. Elsa's just fine.

He stretches his legs out as if he hasn't stretched them for an eternity, so it feels to him.

And the shunting is almost done now, just one loose freight car rolling by. Then there are only the swallows fluttering in and out under the roof.

"But you get so goddamn tired," he says when Pettersson joins him on the seat.

And he doesn't have to answer any questions at all; this shunter is really a gloomy sourpuss. Nowhere nearly so alert as the other railroad fellow, the brakeman under Elsa's window, and not so grateful either.

ROSE OF JERICHO

OF ALL HIS WRITINGS THIS WINTER AND THIS SPRING, AT least one reached its destination; on the last of April it was published in the bi-weekly edition of the *Evening News:*

Cultured Lady
will find rest in country in return
for some help in garden and house-
hold. Reply by letter marked "Tact"
to the office of this newspaper.

On the fifteenth of May she came. By then he was al-most through in the garden, and that was just as well; she didn't look suited for work. She was far too stout for that.

She came toward evening and went to bed early, tired from the journey. But he stayed up long with the other answers, the other pictures. Although, naturally, even she had sent a picture of a round, cheerful face, down to half an inch below the collar—no one could have guessed just from the picture that the rest would be so overwhelming. Naturally he'd had full-length pictures, several of them. But they hadn't really told him very much, nor did they now as he tried to make up his mind whether he had made the wrong choice or not.

A strange moment. In the folding bed above his head his brother had died. A quiet, modest death after a quiet, modest life. Everything had become even more quiet after that—now! now she was turning over, and the ceiling creaked; he felt that the whole house was creaking. Again he stared down into the other answers, again she turned over—and it was like a new fear. He shuddered as if he were doing something forbidden, as if he were being unfaithful to her up there—to her whom he had, after all, settled on for now! He removed the letters and the pictures, removed them quickly—in their place he brought out his almanac and wrote himself to a kind of calm, entered three pencil notes that he had neglected to record while he had been waiting. Blue anemone, April 15; coltsfoot, April 17; daphne, April 25.

"OH THOU CLERK, THOU CLERK, THOU PARISH CLERK. . . ."
But now, of course, he can laugh at that little story. By no manner of means is he to be regarded as a dried-up herb anymore; he himself can see in the mirror that there is a new light in his eyes, a new buoyancy about his shoulders.

For the unexpected happened. Or what he had dreamed about when composing the ad happened. Or quite simply this: that after the night of new fear and new doubt there came a day of self-confidence and contentment.

Several such days.

Of course it's still true that she's not inclined to move much. She has not yet been as far into the garden as the fence, and it doesn't look as if she has any intention of going that far either. And it's exceptional for her to set the table or clear it; on the other hand it's a rule *without* exception that he still does the dishes. And two plates again instead of one, and two soup bowls into the bargain now. And two knives, two forks, two spoons. At coffee time—this, too, was one of the things he had wondered and dreamed about after the ad—at coffee time she would come out with the tray all set; clear over in the square patch where he was fussing around with the medicinal herbs he would hear her woman's voice:

"Coffee's ready!"

It didn't turn out that way. The woman's voice is there, it's there a good deal ahead of the coffee hour, but it says, as she sits there heavy and immovable in his only garden chair, the one his brother bought:

"I'm beginning to feel like a cup of coffee, Kilstadius!"

He has told himself that he is disappointed; at long last he has searched his inner self to find out if he *really* is disappointed. Has rolled over his tongue a reminder about the words in the advertisement concerning help in the home and interest in the garden and herbs—

More and more the desire to voice such a reminder has disappeared and another desire has taken its place; almost every day, bending over the cultivated hyoscyamus and tanacetum, he becomes impatient, looks at his watch several times each half hour, longs to go in to his job of setting the tray. As far as he can see, he has become a real gallant, not the master of the house as he had thought. It was a foolish thought! Less and less does he own up to it, and if the roles had been switched, it seems to him now that his role is not such a bad one—he's been waiting on himself alone long enough!

HE HAS ASKED HER TO READ THE PUBLICATION WHICH CAME as printed matter and which no one but the parish clerk could have sent. *Youth Magazine* is the name of it. And someone has marked with a blue crayon:

"In South America, it is said, there may be found a strange plant which grows only in moist places. In such places it will put down roots and become green for a while until the soil has dried up again. Then it frees itself from the ground, curls up, and is carried by the wind to some other moist place which may be miles and miles away, where the same process is repeated. It keeps on wandering and stopping where there is water until the ground again becomes dry. Finally it is just a bundle of dry roots and dry twigs after all its wanderings."

"That's supposed to be me," he said.

And laughed, now he can laugh.

But she understood nothing, blue-eyed she understood nothing.

"Old—and dry. After all the wanderings."

"But you aren't old, Kilstadius," she said.

She had mentioned something about music. But in passing she had let fall a word about her birthday, on the sixth of June. One week before that he had made up an ad again. It didn't go as far as the *Evening Post;* it just appeared in the local *News.* He took it to the editor himself.

And this time he felt no hesitation in choosing the answer that looked most luxuriant, as it were:

One manual organ, six stops.

THE DRIVER HELPS HIM CARRY THE ORGAN INTO THE LIVING room; then they have a glass of juice in the kitchen—the bus is early and there's only an old woman left in it. He says his guest is a teacher, a school teacher on leave of ab-

sence. She doesn't miss the school, he says, but she misses
music. Now she's having her after-dinner nap.

He begins to polish the organ with a rag.

She plays "Alte Kameraden" so it's like a changing of
the guard right in his house, like a parade in Berlin in the
old days! And he picks up courage from the music; they'll
soon find out whom they've bitten! He is checking off
words in "50,000 foreign-loan words"—abdicate = give up
of one's free will—the honors he never asked for;
abnormal = not following the usual rules—but then he
never has gone along in their grooves; absurd = senseless,
stupid, foolish—that's just what the idea is that he should
therefore be inferior to them in any way; antagonist = foe,
enemy—of two kinds, one of them bigoted = two-faced,
and the other cynical = coarse, unseemly; fiasco = failure,
create a fiasco—well, that may be so; inquiet = uneasy—
is how they will never get to see him anymore—with utter
calm he will stand up against their conspiracy = secret
order!

He doesn't get any further today; much to his surprise
he hears her in the kitchen and rushes down the stairs.
That will never do! Not on her birthday! Gently but
firmly he shoves her out into the garden chair again.

He treats her to a birthday cake; he treats her to a reading aloud from last winter's bulky briefcase:

"The fact that I undertook my journey at such an advanced age completely alone and totally unprepared to
make my way among thieves and bandits in three contin-
ents has aroused considerable amazement and interest in
the countries I traversed. . . ."

She interrupts him, tells him once more he's not so very
old. From the paper rises a little of the agony, the agony
of fear from that evening when he was writing this—is she,

too, one of those who would belittle his contribution? But her eyes are just china-blue; he makes corrections and deletions in his notebook and continues:

"Since, as has already been related, I had been accosted all the way both on my outward and homeward journeys, it was with a certain wondering, indeed almost fear, that I approached my native country where I had suffered so terribly for many decades. I had a small foretaste of what was now about to befall me when I boarded the Swedish ferry at Sassnitz. I was not allowed to buy anything, neither food nor coffee, and got only insolent answers when I asked for something. . . ."

Here he had been unable to write on; from Sassnitz, from Trelleborg, he was suddenly at the home of his relatives:

"They received me so disgracefully," he says now, "so disgracefully that we won't spoil your birthday with that. Only my brother showed that he really thought highly of me for having been able to undertake such a journey. Maybe it wasn't envy that the others felt. . . ."

"Oh yes," she interrupts him again, "of course it was envy."

She becomes animated, quite animated for her:

"It galled them. They were thinking of the money. Anyone can see that such a journey must have cost an awful lot of money."

"ALTE KAMERADEN" AWAKENS HIS MEMORIES—AS SOON AS it started to rain and he rescued the coffee set and the little bit of cake that was left (she had certainly done honor to the cake!) and they have sat down in his room, it becomes the turn of Frau Neumann in Sassnitz.

"Now maybe I can get some help with a letter that I should have sent long ago," he says.

She has told him that she knows a little German.

It's true, he *has* been writing it for several years. But it is of the utmost importance that it should not provide the least opportunity for misinterpretation in any direction— Frau Neumann had tortured his days and nights enough, after all!

He reads in German from a yellowed paper:

"You will without doubt remember that I, the undersigned, spent the night in your hotel while on my way to Jerusalem."

If he reads slowly, she can follow it.

"I have only good things to say about your hotel, but your behavior has made me very...."

"Stories of love affairs," he says. "They tried to make a laughing-stock of me before the whole world with tales of love affairs. I was accosted in every country."

"You conducted yourself in such a way that there can be no doubt that you had heard shameful slander concerning my circumstances...."

"How could this be possible?" he had burst out on sheet after sheet, impotent and trembling. Now he is calmer.

"I must make it clear to Frau Neumann," he says, "that she was not the only one, that it was like this in all of the countries. And that this simply couldn't have happened if it hadn't been for the secret *'conspiracies that exist nowadays'* "—this is the title he has given one of his notebooks. "She shall be forced to confess how she got hold of, where she got hold of all those disgraceful things. I am going to publish the results, and it's going to be of very great interest to certain persons!"

He himself can hear how his voice is soaring up into a treble, but that is really the only similarity to his former outbursts—the organ tones mingled with the cuckoo's call this June make all the old misery appear so distant.

ABOUT ANOTHER PERSECUTION DOWN IN GERMANY, WHEN HE was working on an estate called Frörup twelve miles west of Hadersleben.

"When the owner there reported the arrival of the Swede to the local policeman, he was able to tell him what happened in my childhood."

"Working?" she says. "Were you working, Kilstadius? Weren't you *traveling*?"

There is a little wrinkle across her nose.

"Of course I was traveling," he replies. "I just had to take work to improve my finances. I used to do that quite often."

"I see," she says and looks at him thoughtfully.

In the evening she plays, but not "Alte Kameraden" anymore, rather a song in a gloomy tune, with gloomy words:

The day which just passed will never return—
The law of change does command—
But the deeds that you did are of deepest concern;
In God's Book they are writ by His hand.

The basses among the six stops reinforce retu-u-urn. conce-e-ern—not entirely gloomy, though; he is not alone anymore. Peace, and not just twilight, rests over the garden. But over Frau Neumann in Sassnitz flutters a swarm of the bats of repentance and qualms and fear—

SHE DOESN'T MISS HER SCHOOL YET, SHE SAYS. AND NOW SHE
has her music, too.

"But not many people come here," she says that same
day.

She has moved the garden chair so she can see the road.

That's why he is happy, in spite of the dry herb, when
the parish clerk comes. His errand is to say that alas, alas,
it won't be possible to arrange for a lecture just now. ". . .
you know how it is. People don't want to sit around in-
doors during midsummer."

"But in the fall, Kilstadius, in the fall."

But in the fall might she perhaps be gone?

She doesn't seem to be sorry, however; in her joy she
seems to have forgotten his lecture. She twitters her "cup
of coffee now, Kilstadius," coaxes the parish clerk to take
a seat in the garden chair but so playfully that it is she
herself who drops down into it, as usual.

And of course they are fellow teachers, aren't they, so
they probably have quite a lot to talk about; their voices
drift in to Kilstadius by the stove. It pleases him, indeed it
does, that she has someone to visit with her at long last—it
pleases him that the parish clerk can see what a paradise
he's really got now. And his annoyance at the canceled
lecture—in a way it's good not to have to think about it
anymore; he has finished only the first part.—Three coffee
spoons, three cups, three saucers, a dish for the cookies,
sugar, cream, that's it.

Imagined you now as my bride

.   .   .   .

Imagined you my little wife

it says in his poetry album. "Fantastic Excursions into
Time and Space and into Eternity and Infinity" is going
to be the title of his lecture—he can see the rows of faces
before him, he'll give them something to think about on

their way home in the raw autumn darkness; he'll make the tail of pride droop in each one of them!

"Man's Thought," he has written, "man's Thought, that uneasy roamer, is freer than anything else on earth. Nothing can stop him from making excursions into the times and spaces to which his mistress, the brain, chooses to dispatch him. From a subterranean dungeon he can easily spring up to the regions of the Milky Way, to where only the astronomer can reach with his sine lines."

He has continued in a new notebook, another ten lines: "He moves through time as easily to the days of creation as to the day of doom, lingers in wonder where life was kindled, and flees in terror where it is extinguished. With regard to excursions in time and space, Thought is omnipotent like God himself. In only two cases is he impotent: if he is directed toward the beginning of eternity or toward the ultimate infinity. Then he is seized with giddiness and immediately turns back and wants to stay home, for he can achieve nothing. . . ."

This giddiness he himself has felt. The second lecture is to deal with the journey back, with the world down here:

"When a seasoned person in his mature age casts a critical glance back on his own past life and on the lives of his fellow men without reflecting very deeply on causes and effects, he will easily come to the misleading conviction that Providence perpetrates a barbarous injustice against the sensible beings whom She has assigned to places down here in the valleys of earth, most of which may be called vales of tears. On the one side you see vice and crime triumph and receive an abundance of the gifts of the earth; on the other side you see talented and dedicated persons struggle in vain against poverty and adversity and disease, sinking ever deeper into misery until many of them remain at the bottom of the abyss. Our modern reformers . . . ."

Now the lid of the coffee pot is drumming, drumming like applause. How utterly ignorant is the parish clerk out there, and even if his notebooks will go back into their place on the shelf today too—between a book entitled "The Troubles of the Soul" and a pamphlet he got from an agricultural inspector, "A Few Words About Peat Moss"—they won't remain there long anymore!

"You sure took your time!" she says.

She laughs to the parish clerk.

"But help yourself now!"

HE OVERHEARD THE WORD "ASYLUM" AT THE POST OFFICE. But it wasn't about him; it was about the bride at Haglycka who refuses to get up anymore.

When he gets back home, he is in a bitter mood.

"I, for one, never got any help," he says. "Never any help or friendliness even at the hospital. I have had a lot of experiences both in Stockholm and in the country yet have never been treated with anything but scorn and brutality. This nurses' association . . . ."

Today he says this to provoke her. She has been out for a walk with the parish clerk. She has a cousin who is a nurse.

"There are many kind persons among them," she says. "My cousin is really a very kind person."

"She may well be," he admits. "But still, helping with the blockade!"

All of a sudden his voice rises to a screaming pitch, and his cheeks turn red.

"Can't you see that that's why I went to Jerusalem! To put an end to that blockade! At least the one against me personally! I wrote a pamphlet. I sold nineteen copies, that's all; there are four hundred and eighty-one left up there in the attic!"

And now he continues in the words of the pamphlet; he knows them by heart:

"Any scoundrel can treat me just as he likes. Here at home they tried again and again to have me committed for persecution mania."

He tosses his head and upper body backward:

"Nobody dared to start writing in earnest, though! Just shouting, 'Crucify him, crucify him, and give us Barrabas!' Why, in the first house I entered in Germany . . . ."

"Frau Neumann," she says, and her voice trembles.

He can hear that she is scared, but now he is going to prove to her once and for all how far-reaching the ramifications and organization of this persecution are! She's not going to hide behind the parish clerk! He strides up and down the room; now he is lecturing to her about the gang of card sharps and crooks in Barcelona. About the Sociedad de la Innocenza, the protectors of innocence, in the horrible black dresses and high conical hats with slits for the eyes and mouth. "A similar gang rose up in America, with the only difference that their ghastly garb was snow white as a symbol of their noble work—which was murder and crime! The Ku Klux Klan. . . ."

She stares at him, terrified.

"Haha!" he laughs, carried away with her fear, with his own fear. "And now we shall soon get to the parish clerk. The Ku Klux Klan was banned, but the members organized themselves instead as the Independent Order of Good Templars! A scoundrel by the name of Hickman! In due time this order got to Sweden and introduced the secret blockade upon Swedish soil!"

As the words are spoken, he feels the thick lines under

the words in his notebook; he underlines them once more in the air with a mighty sweep of his right hand.

"And this blockade is so secret that only a few Good Templars know about it; all the others have no idea of the company they are in! That is what is so dangerous and terrifying. But they are useful all the same, for they help to spread degrading gossip about the unhappy persons who are victims of the blockade. The parish clerk is such a gossip monger. . . ."

Again all his confidence collapses—the cancellation of his lecture is proof of the deceitfulness of confidence, the letter to Professor Gadelius to which he never got a reply is proof, the seed potatoes he had to wait for till the middle of May, till the day before she arrived—further proof!

She tells him that those are trifles, little coincidences, quite harmless little events—oh! he has the answer; he takes a sentence from a notebook where he has collected the "Sayings of Great Men": "What merely scratches the nail of one penetrates into the innermost heart of another and burns like poison!"

IN THE EVENING SHE SINGS:

> I sometimes wish that I
> A winging dove might be,
> O'er deserts' sandy wastes to fly
> From perils hastily.

And in the morning, when the mowing machines are rattling again, the dove is winging away. By the first bus. Not to the sandy wastes, just to her cousin. O'er deserts' sandy wastes, instead, who flew o'er deserts' sandy wastes?

Cast about by the winds? The dry herb. Or else what did the parish clerk mean?

When evening comes again, he takes a walk to the churchyard and back. He does not meet anyone, stops at the wall of a stable and throws his water. Then he hears the horse inside sighing. A long, heavy sigh.

GATEPOST

" '...DAMNED IF SHE AIN'T GONNA CALVE TODAY,' I SAID. 'You can see that all right, can't you?' I said. 'And just imagine what it'd be like to have them standing in the cowshed bawling,' I said. 'Especially now that it's getting to be warmer...' "

(... warmer? On the contrary there's a cold draught here. And these new jerseys are just a lot of junk, he's felt all day long. He felt that when he bought them—that they were thin and sleazy.

And as if he had no greater worry than that the jerseys were getting thinner and poorer quality, he's taking it easy here with this other fellow. Skoots his hat back on his neck and scratches his bald spot.

And this is a newfangled thing too, not having much hair left; last fall the comb began to rake off bigger and bigger tufts of his grey mop. Then it went quickly; now there's just skin left and a little fuzz on top of his crown. In spots there's not even any fuzz.

And so the pitiful relief of scratching and scratching his hair was denied him; only last night it was denied him when he made up his mind to take the trip to the doctor.

Scratched as if he wanted to tear off the skin after the hair.

Now he feels the fine velvet hat right against his fingers; he is raking about in the brim because a man has to have something to do.)

" '...so just let her go along with the others,' I said. 'You can bet she'll be coming back,' I said. And she came back in the evening. The poor thing. And sure as hell she'd had her calf anyway, went and stood by a birch tree and lapped up the afterbirth. The other beasts were there too and did their bit. But there wasn't a trace of the goddamn calf . . ."

(Raking around and drawing in the nap as if he were writing something.

Same as he sat writing last night until he himself saw how desolate it appeared. Then he grabbed the fly swatter as if to give chase—but went on sitting and scribbling even with the swatter. Choppy little bits as his thoughts came and went choppily. Is any more proof needed—proof that he's ill—than that on an evening in early June he could be sitting waving a fly swatter which had been shoved around the table all this winter?

Up to now it had gone to the pantry, at any rate, when the summer was over.

But this year and last year he had been in such pain that the objects in his home just turned into lead around him; everything, down to the smallest knickknacks, became as heavy as the heaviest pieces of furniture.)

". . . and the women took to hollering and carrying on, of course. 'Where's the calf now?' they said. 'How the hell do I know,' I said. It was getting pretty dark by now. 'And there's no goddamn point in looking for it either,' I said. 'Because when a damned cow ups and runs away from a calf just like that, you can be sure we won't find it tonight,' I said. 'Let's wait till morning instead and she'll probably go back to him on her own,' I said . . . ."

(Supposing the city doctor had made a mistake? He thought of that a while ago—and whistled a little. It isn't his habit to whistle as he walks, or at any rate it hasn't been in a long time.)

"... they tried to make her go along with them for a ways. They didn't get very far before she turned and started loping back. It was night for her like for the rest of them. She wanted to be inside the cowshed. . . ."

(But he'd rather—yes, he'd much rather look a bit silly perhaps than have them sense the verdict.

Then he stopped in the middle of the road and told himself that, "Anyway you aren't going to die today, you know."

He's to be tortured first. Tortured long? The whole summer, half the winter maybe?

It doesn't make any difference whether he whistled or not. Whether he whistles tomorrow, or the day after tomorrow. They'll get to know the verdict. And then they'll be keeping their eyes on him. Look to see if he's really coming out today—the today three or four months from now.

If he's really coming out in the morning and standing there scratching himself, completely at a loss and ill. When he can barely drag himself over the threshold.

Evald at Lugnet, he crawled at the end. Crawled out to the woodshed, got up on his knees, and chopped a few sticks.

Until one morning he didn't come out of the door anymore.)

" '... well, you can see that plain enough,' I said. 'Now give up on that she-devil,' I said. And of course they had to whether they wanted to or not because she was halfway to the cowshed by now. 'What *have* you done with the calf,' they whined. 'Maybe there'll be a thunderstorm to-night!' they cried."

(Though of course for some the final day has come fast enough. And maybe he's gotten through some of the waiting time already—with the pains he's had?

For even if he isn't as sick as the doctor had made out, had written a letter about, still he has certainly grown old.)

". . . but it's sure odd how some just leave them. I lay there and thought about that for a while, because it was downright impossible to sleep. Whether it was because of the thunderstorm or because of the calf. . . ."

(Doesn't eat well. Sleeps even worse. Knows a thing or two himself about finding it downright impossible to sleep.

In past years he could get along on little food and he could always fall asleep, used to sleep extra good after days more hellish than usual.

It's different now. Of course, he always feels sleepy at the old "children's hour," and it frequently happens that he dozes off in the chair where he's sitting.

But once he gets into bed, everything is as if be-witched.

Then he just lies there staring.

He can buy food although he doesn't work every day; crowns keep piling up without his quite understanding how it happens—he's especially well stocked with two-crown pieces and yet he handed out a whole lot of them when he bought himself this new outfit for the trip to the doctor.

It's the same no matter what he tempts himself with.

He has tried the most curious cans at the grocery store; still he has no taste for any of them.

Part of it he just vomits up again—no earthly good it's done him. Occasionally he throws up his food several times a day.)

"... so at the first crack of dawn I went out and untied her, and then we headed up into the hills. I had a bit of a drop of something in a bottle...."

(He used to be able to hold his liquor and get good and drunk. Now that pleasure too is over; he tried at Christmas, he tried on his birthday. Both times he felt just plain miserable.

Today he didn't go into the liquor store.)

"... but she was just nibbling off a little grass here and there. She didn't seem to give a damn that we were out to find the calf she'd dropped. 'Is it this way?' I said. 'Is this the way we go?' I said...."

(For that matter, he has owned up to people about the bad taste of liquor. He's been carrying on almost like a prohibition-preacher—"How can you swallow that bilge," he's been saying.)

"... then we tore off up that damned steep slope, you know, and when the brush got really thick, she just ran on that much faster, so I thought this must surely be the right way and ran along too...."

(He is swallowing something else in his loneliness. But that he does not talk about. Swallowing tears. He cries quite often.)

" '... well, where the hell have you got the calf now?' I said. ...."

(Do all old people become like him, crying and swallowing? But supposing they aren't sick, supposing they don't have any *symptoms?* When Johan at Lerdal got cancer, he had stood in the store one day and said that the symptoms were just like when his sister got it, and he had had tears in his voice. As if he had just been crying or was going to cry as soon as he could get out and be alone again.)

"... she stopped and rubbed herself against a scrub pine. 'Is it here?' I said. Then she put her muzzle to the ground and began to graze again. ...."

(What will *he* say in the store today? Or some day later on—if he is up to walking over there? Just how sick will he be by then?)

"... then I let her walk for a while. I'd gotten up a little too early. I was tired and sleepy. I curled up under a fir tree. She had a bell, of course. ...."

("What difference does it make," he'll say. "One old codger more or less."
That Aina in the store. Rosy cheeks and an overflowing bosom.
It happens that he imagines his worn-out paws way down inside that blouse opening of hers—last winter when the weather was at its coldest.
But they damned well stayed put on the edge of the counter; if they pinched anything, it would be just the loaf of bread she had put there, and the roll of tobacco which he still bought just out of habit although it tasted

like manure, and the goat cheese, and the bag of oatmeal, and half a kilo of farm butter. Sad to say, you left that dazzling bosom of hers alone.)

" '. . . did you leave it way over yonder?' I said. . . ."

(Alone. Of course, he's got a brother up in Norrland and one in America if he's still alive. The last letter had been three years ago last Easter.

A trip to Norrland, a trip to America will be equally out of the question from now on. They'll stay where they are, and he'll stay where he is.)

". . . it wouldn't be devilish enough otherwise, I thought, and traipsed after . . ."

(Try to write them. Instead of just sitting here waving the fly swatter? To tell them they are cordially welcome to the funeral.)

". . . and there I found her at long last. But no calf. 'Well, let's go home!' I said. 'Clod!' I said. 'Goddamn cow . . .' "

(Knowing nothing ahead of time. He wanted to know if there was only a smidgen of time left.

"No one can tell," the doctor had answered.

Sometime this fall. Sometime during the winter. Or next spring? Clear till fly-swatter time again?)

". . . I said. 'Let's go home and get some people,' I said. And it was just as if she had figured that it was too early for her to be up too and now she wanted to go home and sleep, for all of a sudden she bounded off. I barely had time to see her rump and a brown and white blur and hear a little tinkle. But after that she might have gone up in smoke for all that I heard or saw of her. Heard only that damned cuckoo calling. . . ."

(It could take *years.* Berta at Kyrkbraten lay in bed for two years. More than two years.)

". . . get some people and go hunting for a newborn calf in the pouring rain. I just said that to her for a joke. . . ."

(One summer night in his youth. She had her young man already but then that jackass got stoned; she pushed and tugged at him for a while. All of a sudden she let him lie there, straightened up, and eyed the others. "*You* go in with me," she said. A nice place, even a top sheet that he got himself tangled up in. Half a night. Then never again. There came her marriage to that sot of hers and a young-ster shortly afterward.)

". . . cow or no cow and calf or no calf. . . ."

(He remembers she died on a market day, the last mar-ket day that he went to with a horse and ended up with the police; those goddamn troublemakers thought he was drunk just because he went down the street bareheaded with a stallion that was determined to walk on two legs.)

". . . running like a madman just for the sake of a stupid cow. And I was so wet I could wring the water out of my duds. 'Here, girl,' I said. 'Here, cow,' I said. 'Co', Boss. C'mere,' I said. . . ."

(What had happened to his hat? Neither he nor the police could find it.)

"... then I caught sight of her again. ..."

(And he trudged home bareheaded next evening. Then the white curtains had been pinned together at Kyrk-braten and there were lights burning both upstairs and downstairs.

He lost almost a whole winter's earnings at that market. But did he cry because of that? Or for Berta?

Now he has a wet handkerchief in his pocket even on weekdays. There are so many tears that he can't squeeze them away with just his fingers.)

"... oh, yes, she was homeward bound. Jogging and jumping downhill, so content, so heartily content. ..."

(He fingers the doctor's sealed letter to the hospital. Once before he had clenched such a letter between his fingers, when it was about Holger and the sanitorium. But the boy never got that far; he was allowed to die at home.

Tonight he is going to hold his own death sentence up to the light and look at the sheet inside the envelope. One always thinks he is going to be able to read what's there.

Not to hit upon a single thought that won't be linked with the thought of leaving. From now on all his musings will slip out and glide along in that forever-same stream.)

" '... wait a minute,' I said. 'Can't you hear me?' I said, and I, too, began to run harder again. Running and curs-ing like nothing you've ever heard before. 'Well, there'll be hell to pay,' I hollered into the forest, 'if I'm not going to make that she-devil of a cow find her calf ....' "

(There will be long nights—long, aching, silent nights. Extra-long nights, as Berta had said.

Did *she* lie there thinking about what the nights had been like once? For that's what they believe, isn't it, these young women, that it's going to be one big joy ride.

Emma probably thought so. He and she had kept hard at it and panted right through a Whitsuntide once; Holger came of that. The next kid was—well, in even more of a hurry, smiled and turned back, as his boss, the forester, wrote in the obituary.)

". . . but then it was as if she had finally understood what we were chasing after. She looked a lot more sensible now. We pressed on into a bog. But no. She came out of there again and began to lumber along quite slowly. . . ."

(The last time Emma came from the sanitorium she was just to keep quiet, they told her. Preferably no work at all. But of course the washtub had no legs of its own to walk on. Emma was not yet fifty on the evening she lay slumped head first over the lip of the well. She thought she was going to live; she had bought herself some false teeth which came in the mail and which he had been obliged to pay for when he went to order the coffin.)

". . . the winter road, you know . . ."

(The kids were of the same stamp, none of them left. Yet stubborn in their way, like their mother. "Eat!" he had told Holger one evening. "Eat the food that's on the table. It's good enough." He didn't eat. Another guy might have given him a wallop, but his father never dared to; he was too strong. Just hoisted him outside the door: "Stand there until you're hungry!" He had on nothing but a shirt and it was five degrees outside. But he stayed on. He was blue when he was allowed to come in again for Emma's sake after she'd been whining for about an hour. He didn't eat then either.)

"... down through the forest by the vicarage. Straight down the middle of the road. Having a fine time. Didn't seem to care much for the grass anymore and was in no hurry at all. And then she stopped by a fir tree and there was the calf standing under the tree ..."

(Quickly into the grave now, that would be something! Slither down into the coffin and pull the lid over yourself.)

"... standing up and looking at me with the most beautiful eyes you could imagine. And of course he was hungry, poor little thing. But just listen to this! Do you think that bitch would let him get at her! Here comes the little one shoving his head in toward the udder, but right then he gets a kick that sends him flying for two or three meters at least. ..."

Johannes Åsbom is walking backward now to pace off how far the calf was thrown.

At the same time his listener steps out into the road again and touches his velvet hat lightly.

"It was a good thing," Åsbom tells his womenfolk over the supper potatoes. "It was a good thing I had this story about the calf to take his mind off it. Because of course I could see it right away. I could see perfectly well what the doctor had told him."

THE WHITSUN BRIDE

SHE IS OUT OF BED AGAIN AND STANDS WAITING WITH HER mother for the Monday morning bus; she's going in to the doctor to get some cough medicine. She is cold and shivering and still has a fever; after all, the weather is pretty chilly even now. But they are talking to Elvira, the seamstress, about materials and about helping with the sewing before the holidays.

But the bus is late; once everything goes black for Karin, and she almost crumples rather than sits down on the edge of the ditch. They have a car at their house, to be sure, and obviously it might have come in handy now—it just happens to be springtime for her father, too. He rushed off with the car as usual last Saturday night and hasn't come back yet.

". . . a flowered voile. . . ."

But when the bus still doesn't show up, they talk quite angrily for a while about the car and about the fool man who stays away half a week at a time, more and more often now.

They come back on the last bus. The one with the fewest passengers.

Baffled.

Frightened.

"Empty-handed-like," says Elvira.

Although they had both the cake box and flowers and the material.

And completely openhearted, suddenly completely openhearted with what little they have to tell.

Baffled because there's no more.

"Home and to bed!" was all he had said. "Right away. Damned if I know how this will end up."

He had been at his very roughest; yet he got rough like that only when a life was at stake, didn't he—that's what seems so absurd, that's why they give themselves plenty of time for the kilometer they have to go from the crossroads home.

They had done just the same in town, had sat cowering for almost three hours in the eating house before they took the emptiest bus.

But he surely couldn't have meant it like that. When he didn't even keep her in there at the hospital—

"Where they're lying like sardines in a can," says Elvira.

And that may be so. But when he gave them some medicine and told her expressly that she must stay home, he couldn't possibly have meant that she was simply—

". . . going to die?"

They can see that people start at this. And that's exactly why Betty, her mother, takes this word into her mouth, takes it exorcisingly into her mouth. Merely to hear again, to let them hear, how absurd, how just plain absurd it sounds.

Because of course Karin is going to pull through. As long as she takes her medicine and gets herself back to bed.

Supposing she really had danced herself to death?

They said the whole crazy trip was actually her idea. Her eager idea. Again and again she had wriggled in and out of the grasp of the new truck driver, given him soft drinks at the store, moved the cigarette from his mouth to hers—Saturday morning he was free, took the day off and nailed together some benches on the back of the truck.

But then around evening it became so cold that just

one bench was enough, and there was room left even on that. It was more than thirty miles away, and now that the dancing pavilion here at Tallmon would be opening on the coming holiday anyway, several of them were hesitant about going. Both she and the truck driver urged them; it took a lot of time, and she finally got two girls to go only on the condition that they could sit up in the cab.

A thin blouse and a thin summer coat, dancing and sweating until the next morning, and riding all the way home on the open back of the truck—when the hoar frost lay white on the fields.

Well, she had really felt that she was sort of the organizer and responsible for the greatest possible amount of fun. And kicked against the pricks.

THE GROUND HAS THAWED AT LAST. THE WOMEN STAY OUT-doors longer and longer each time—they can see each other as they putter and rake and tidy up.

Can see each other particularly well this morning since they are aware that the thoughts of all are on the same track; move in closer to the fence so they can be within earshot.

"How high is it today? Have you heard anything?"

"Nothing yet today. But yesterday it was a hundred and three point six."

Last night a little echo drifted along the ridge; sure, they heard it—about that high temperature. Temperature, the echo repeated, almost a hundred and four. A hundred and four.

But today? Had anything happened during the night? For a short while the voices are edged with impatience until they return to last night's tidings about how ill she was.

What does Elvira know, down in the road on her bicycle?

"What have you heard, Elvira?"

She doesn't slow down; she just yells out one word in reply.

"Better."

The point behind this one little word is that Elvira considers it enough for Lina who still hasn't let on about her pay for the day-work she did at potato-time last fall, enough for Elin for her constant gibes about the new preacher, enough for Signe because of that old love story.

All three of them know this as they stand there following the bicycle with their eyes.

Later on, when Elvira alights farther up the valley, where she doesn't begrudge the people a fuller account, she says that of course Karin might be a little better. Seeing as how the temperature has dropped.

But that's not much to rely on anymore.

The real news is rather that a letter has been sent to Karin's fiancé, poor fellow, telling him to come home from his military service.

That's how sick she really is.

Soon after Elvira the doctor's car drives by.

Is there. Was there.

Is gone.

All according to the echo for the time being.

THE NEXT DAY THE PORCH DOOR IS OPEN FOR THE PREACHER. But not on the following day; Karin has less fever now, but she is awfully tired—he treated her a bit too violently, treated them all a bit too violently. He got a revival meeting going that made the walls ring around the sick girl and around the family and around the half dozen women he had dragged along.

"This can't be doing any good," says Mr. Haglund and stays home from his store.

And shuts the porch doors.

"You're shutting out Jesus," Betty wails.

But Haglund is fiercely desperate now; there is murder in his eyes.

So she gives in.

Instead the Sunday school teacher turns up. He is milder; he doesn't hold a meeting but sits quietly by the drawn blind and talks about the Christmas parties at the schoolhouse that Karin used to go to. Talks as if to himself about the candles and the winter apples.

Both Betty and Karin fall asleep while he is sitting there.

THE SOCCER CLUB IS HANGING AROUND AT THE CROSSROADS IN the evening when her fiancé gets there.

He seems kind of dazed, shy and scared when he tries to pass on to them—

"Jesus has said. . . ."

But he, for one, can't stand this salvation business, he says.

"If I hadn't left. . . ."

As if running away from something:

"I wouldn't have been able to stand against it either . . . ."

The soccer club shivers inwardly, not because of the

breeze that passes through the young birch leaves, but because he confides in them so mawkishly and so openly all of a sudden. So lost, so without a foothold—it's as if he were floating in mid-air as he holds up the ring to them:

"She gave it back to me!"

Shy and alien to her eagerness for salvation—but they in turn are shy and alien to him now. None of them can offer any help, if that's what he wants. Some of them think of the truck driver instead, and a suspicion of a smile hovers about their lips.

Then he looks so forsaken, so utterly forlorn and miserable in his private's uniform.

The preacher pedals by on his bike.

And a little later the Sunday school teacher's youngest daughter. She has been away this winter; now she's coming into bloom and has a short skirt and round, silken legs.

She has been saved, by nature kind of, that girl. But she'll be a beauty anyway.

All of them stare after her. The fiancé is just the first to take his eyes off her again.

The Sunday school teacher rides by. From his high seat he looks victoriously down into the soccer club, straight down into the breast of the poor fiancé.

So death is coming, up the hills—coming—

Turn back! Turn back! Surely there is no sense in this; she hasn't lived yet; come again another year and take one of us first—

Haglund says that if Karin may live he will—

He is left standing with an armful of promises, a heavy load of them that no one accepts.

The next day he says that if she dies, he doesn't know what he might—

An armful again, of big, dark threats now.

But no one yields. The promises are dust, the threats nothing but dust.

Betty Haglund, on the other hand, is making friends with death. He is going to stay here, she can see, and so her home will be his home. His home and the home of Jesus. Success, in the eyes of the world, has been theirs all these years, but that was not success in her eyes. And for a little while she takes the reins out of Haglund's helpless hands and puts them into the hands of the preacher. He enters through the porch door again on the next to last day of Karin's life.

They become small, both of them become children again as this stranger with a scythe moves in close to them—sits about where the Sunday school teacher was sitting day before yesterday. They don't look his way, but he gets to hear how poor and lonesome they are—that they don't really have anything but this flowered voile for the Whitsun dress. Karin has the material with her in the bed and is stroking it with her hand, a hand that is so pale and so tired.

And Betty tries a feeble story, a miserably feeble little story:

"I'll have it with me," she says. "When I come to you in Heaven, I'll have the voile with me."

BUT THEN TIME GROWS SHORT FOR ALL THIS. ". . . BEGONE, oh, begone at last thou earthly bridegroom; despite everything the spirit could not get a hold on him. Room only for Jesus. And now is the accepted time," is the preacher's text.

So she is saved during those final hours, those few final hours; again there are prayers and singing all around her.

Joyful singing, as time wears on.

And amid the rejoicing a message from the deathbed to the young people of this countryside, who during the noon hour have to submit to her being their superior for a little while by virtue of her election.

The message of the Creator in the days of thy youth.

They squirm a little, and their cheeks flush over the pork and the potatoes—it could just as easily have been one of them. They still don't give a damn about the preacher, and it'll stay that way, but this greeting straight from her—

Frisky at the dances, frisky off in the alder bushes—

And how quickly the blushing cheek may turn chalky white, how quickly the girl who was just playing around may be called to the reckoning.

A greenish-blue aureole seems to shimmer around the one or two little pieces they remember from the Sunday school magazine, seems to radiate around the verse in their confirmation Bible.

But as the evening wears on, the tales die away one after the other. Now there's only talk of a wreath, and that it will be an expensive wreath. This is the most expensive flower time to die at.

"Karin is happy," says Elvira. Who shrouded her. And made her as beautiful as a Whitsun bride.

And could anyone have imagined a finer day for passing?

"Yes, Karin is happy. . . ."

But already, one by one, the thoughts go a little farther away than just to the churchyard. To other plans for the summer which really seems to have come at last, other plans than just a funeral.

"Karin is happy...."

Not so far away either, maybe no farther than tomorrow. And then her happiness is—"Well, I suppose we may state it thus," as the minister usually expresses himself, "then her happiness is of the kind you would gladly do without in spite of the beauty of the moment."

Just for the sake of the beauty of the moment.

Once more a day of life.

And the truck driver from the evening of the dance is who drives her now too, on the spruce-lined back of the truck. Anyway he has his own problems to think about; last Saturday he was drunk and drove the truck into a newsstand, so now he has to go to jail this summer. For the present he still has his license; Haglund and the sheriff have agreed that he may keep it through today.

Haglund has been crying, and soon he will be crying again. But for a brief moment—while they are waiting for the minister, and Johan Bäckman is pausing with his elbows on the metal sill of the belfry window to rest himself between the first and second ringings of the bells—at that moment with clear eyes Haglund inspects the crowd that has assembled. As far as he can see, no one is missing. This does honor to Karin, but it does honor also to the store—there are people present whom the minister can't get down here even for the Christmas Day service, but they are on Haglund's books and now they are here. He gives Betty's arm a little squeeze—considering things practically, she need not be so completely disconsolate.

True enough, Karin should not have passed away. But she is not the only one they have, is she? There are four more youngsters, all of them quite good in their own ways.

The only one that looks a trifle seedy is the fiancé, he reflects. But tomorrow his furlough will be over, so then he won't be hanging around here anymore.

For a month or so.

And by then the worst should be over.

Follow her right up to the strange, spruce-lined hole. No farther. Betty alone among them wishes to go beyond at this moment.

Now for the honors. With all these young people who have gathered together for the choir. With the procession which forms in such fine and regular order that it would seem we had never done anything but march in lines like this. With a parish clerk who has washed the classroom chalk off himself so his big fat ears shine with the sunlight passing through them. And with a minister who—"Oh, *good enough!*" as Haglund himself had uttered in English when that persistent man of God succeeded in getting elected to this parish.

Yes, we do well as a team as long as something really solemn harnesses us together. In everyday life we each try our own little path now and then, and for the most part it doesn't look like much—there it happens that we bump against a fence or drive into the ditch. But along this common road, the only certain road, there we manage as well as the most experienced undertaker. We are living in an out-of-the-way place here but that doesn't mean that we have to ask for help. And especially if He who dwells on high helps us by giving us a day as lovely as this!

Then of course it is true that there is never an excess of loveliness; Providence has taken care of that. When the service is over and we are trotting homeward along the three other roads—all of us who don't have something to rake over and set straight in the churchyard—then the sun disappears behind a cloud again, but only so that the dry north wind can get really icy; there won't be any rain today either.

And look how poor the grass is—

BACHELOR PARTY

JUST AS HE'D KEPT SAYING TO HIMSELF:

"I get so nervous, I really do. When there's something the matter with me. . . ." So he says it once more, excusingly, when he is back out on the hospital steps.

Now, when there's nothing wrong with his kidneys. And the trip to town consequently unnecessary.

He doesn't go down to the beer parlor at the brewery and sit; he goes into a sporting goods store and looks at skis, children's skis for the stepdaughter he's going to get. He doesn't stop to think that she has a bad hip which makes her limp until there is a sales clerk with him telling him the prices.

That's remarkably much money just for two simple boards.

Then he thinks he might chat a little with this clerk, tell him that she still has a bad hip which makes her limp, but that it'll probably pass some day. Or tell him that, when all was said and done, he himself was in good health, that there was nothing wrong with his kidneys as he'd kept imagining—he begins to long for a chance to talk. "Pee," was about all the doctor had said. "Pee in this glass," and apart from that he had been all but dumb during the whole time of pressing and pissing and pressing again.

But the sales clerk doesn't look interested either, stands and stares off toward some other customers.

Then his mood suddenly takes a new tack. By golly, they don't have to sell him any skis at all; he'll see to that!

And he certainly doesn't say it rudely. Through his resentment he still feels that he owes some gratitude on account of his kidneys; the skis were meant to be just that, a token of gratitude—he says politely but insincerely:

"What time do you close this evening?"

"At six."

The clerk wakes up after all, notices his existence, says once more:

"We close at six."

It's just a little after two now.

"I'll be back a little later then."

"All right," the clerk replies trustingly.

"IT'LL SURE BE SOME PARTY," SAYS ROLLÉN, THE STOREKEEP-er. "He carried his lunchbox pretty heavy-like, I noticed."

He had seen Åman getting off the bus.

One liter is on them, but just one on all of them put together. That makes their share uneven, and so in some confusion they also buy the flowery plates which properly go with the flowery tureen.

Although later on it becomes less uneven as they go along balancing this idiotic load on the icy road for his sake.

And still less as they won't be able to say something like, "It's a good wife you're getting, Åman."

They can't possibly do that.

Anyway, they have come out of the forest tired, and back into the forest they'll have to go tomorrow. This is no Saturday night.

And there she sits—

Sits stock still on the sled, although it's about fifteen degrees outside.

And stares at the bright window.

"Why, good evening," they say.

"Good evening."
You can just barely hear it.
"Aren't you cold?"
"Oh, no."
They go on inside.
"There's a female sitting out there. . . ."
Åman swings his feet down off the sofa-back into a pair
of new galoshes.
"Could it be your fiancée? We weren't quite sure, but I
think so. . . ."
Åman dashes out.
But he comes right back again.
"Yup," he says. "And it sure was just in the nick of
time. . . ."
It isn't quite clear if he means that she's frozen stiff or
that she had intended to take off. And, indeed, he goes
over to the stove now and pours out some coffee from the
pot into a thermos, but then he lets it stand there open,
without putting the cork in; he doesn't hurry out. Instead
he goes from the stove up to his room. Then they can
hear him down through the ceiling, can hear that he's
changing, that he's over in the closet rummaging about
again and taking the shoetrees out of his boots.
He looks real snappy when he comes down, but he's in
no hurry, no hurry at all; he takes time out to tell them
what he pretends is unknown to them—that she hardly
ever does say very much.
"No, she hardly ever does. Hardly ever does say very
much," he repeats sort of to himself.
"She's awfully shy," he says louder.
He doesn't go until they say to him point-blank:
"You'd damn well better go and give her that coffee
now! If that's what you meant to do. . . ."

They poke fun at him for a while when they're alone.

"That goddamn farmhand," they say. "'Who isn't like ordinary people."

And poke fun at each other for rushing over here in the middle of the week. But then they probably wouldn't have had so much fun even on a Saturday night.

Stick more conversation barbs into Åman's destiny. About the little girl he's getting into the bargain, through no fault or merit of his own but rather through the work of a road laborer, about six or seven years ago. The guy that finally put dynamite between his teeth when he ran into nothing but child welfare workers whichever way he turned.

The whole back of his scalp splattered against the wall of the barracks.

Further, they say:

"Well, we'll see. If Master Åman isn't making things unnecessarily complicated for himself. . . ."

Has made them complicated already.

They also think, think they've noticed, that sometimes it's as if he wanted to be admired somehow, as if he had a *right* to some sort of admiration.

They talk about that time just before Christmas, the eve of St. Lucia. The kids had suddenly got a new school mistress and were to be there an hour earlier in the morning to sing songs and walk around carrying lighted candles.

That was the first time anyone had seen Edit standing and gaping outside Åman's window.

A QUARTER OF AN HOUR, TWENTY MINUTES HAVE PASSED when he returns. But it looks as if he really doesn't see them at all now.

Rather, as if he were still out there on the road, across the darkness.

Until he says:

"She's awfully modest. . . ."

This is probably well meant, but it sounds stupid, terribly stupid, they feel. Supposing the road laborer had said the same thing once upon a time. "Modest. . . ."

"Though of course she's a bit empty-headed too," he says then.

And after he's been silent once more:

"Sometimes she's scared, she says."

Again he stands gazing at something beyond them.

"Scared that something bad is going to happen to me. . . ."

Good Lord! they think then. When he has chosen a life together with this miserable little bit of a wife-to-be, nothing else bad can happen to him! Because that's enough; the devil doesn't ask for more.

"There was nothing wrong with my kidneys. . . ."

For the fourth or fifth time this evening he is back on the hospital steps, is walking down them, is passing up the beer parlor, is in the sporting goods store.

"They're probably going to do some wondering in there," he says. "Why I never came back like I said I would."

But with a spasmodic attempt to be a more interesting host at last, he says:

"Just imagine that I got to be thirty-five after all."

And he explains that all last summer and all fall and around Christmas he hadn't believed he'd make it—he is letting his loneliness and worry and defenselessness last that long now—

Because liquor-driven sadness is throbbing in him in spite of the tureen with the gorgeous roses.

"How about taking a little better look at that," Albert suggests when he has followed Åman's gaze.

And Åman replies meekly:

"Yup. She's bound to like it. . . ."

But it's not *her* opinion Albert wants, and he thinks this liquor tastes bad and so the gift of china becomes of much more worth than Åman's bottles.

He becomes obstinate; it's Åman's opinion that he wants!

Åman senses the other's awakening anger and does as well as he can by the china service:

"We don't have much of anything yet, as you know . . . ."

Somehow this sounds belittling; does he perhaps mean that they haven't brought enough presents—

"Just speak up, will you!" Borggren thunders. "So we can. . . ."

But this in its turn sounds too abrupt; Albert puts one hand over Borggren's mouth. Because Åman surely didn't mean anything of the kind.

"I meant . . ."

For the sixth time!

". . . now that I know there's nothing wrong with my kidneys. Everything's going to turn out all right, I guess . . . ."

All of a sudden he's yelling:

"That's why, don't you see? Just out of gratitude. The skis. . . ."

He breaks off just as suddenly, silently fills glass after glass to overflowing. Now he's barely heard as he mutters:

"Because I just get so nervous. When I start thinking . . . ."

"Oh hell, stop worrying about those damned kidneys," Albin yells almost as loud as Åman a while ago.

"Let's drink to that," agrees Manuel.

"Yes, drink up, Åman," says Albert. "You drink up, too!"

Says this warmly.

Warmly, smoothing out all harm.

BUT ALREADY BORGGREN IS SAYING:

"Well, thanks, Åman. Thanks for the evening."

And burps sourly, or more like an upwelling from joyless liquor and more snuff than usual. With a closing thud of his glass against the oilcloth, he turns from the party to the coming day:

"I'll be damned if those cursed pit props won't have to...."

At last a topic of conversation that can outdo a farmhand's pair of healthy kidneys.

And how late everything will be in the forest this year.

Åman has no forest. But he is stubborn in his faith that he"ll get one—he has even sent a five-crown note to the bearded fortune-teller in Holland.

Rox Roy. Emmastraat. den Haag.

"Bright," it states incontrovertibly on the typewritten papers. That the future is bright. "Luck in love," it says, "and a lucky event." And finally, "Money to be earned," and that couldn't very well be anything but a forest deal.

"Bright...."

But of course reality doesn't look like that; it indisputably does not look like that. Reality, that's either taking over the farm of his father-in-law, a bad tenant farm—and continuing his loud inner voice, he begins to tell them over again things they've known much longer than he:

that those are really pretty worthless people he's being saddled with—or, and this would be better, he supposes (appealing for their support, for their interest this one time!) —

"...would be better, having those old folks come to stay here as kind of lodgers...."

He means that he might try just as well now as later to get this farm on tenancy. This farm where he's a hired hand now. He's been offered this, although on pretty hard terms.

"Bring 'em here, both the old fogey and the wretched old biddy—Especially since this mute bride of mine—Well, she just can't imagine herself being separated from them...."

He gets no answer.

Then he gets angry again, suddenly—they can good and well have an opinion about this! They can good and well listen for a while! After all it's he who's supplying the liquor! At least they can *listen!* About the load he'll have to pull—"It'll be a damned sight worse than your pit props...."

Yells. And his voice sounds neighing and tearful all at the same time.

WHEN HE HAS FILLED THE GLASSES UP AGAIN AND THERE isn't much left in the last bottle, they back him into a corner, way into a corner. "Free liquor is one thing, and thanks for that, Åman! But if a farmhand—an ordinary farmhand even if he hails from another parish—if he makes things unnecessarily complicated for himself, like we were saying while you were out, and then thinks he's going to be admired into the bargain, now that's quite another thing, Åman! This kid, for example, that can't even walk right yet. . . ."

"Well, you're taking over, you sure are, Åman," says Borggren as he swaggers off and spits a quid of snuff into the sink.

"I hope you've thought it through," underlines Manuel, who now is coming out of his drunken state in some strange way.

Åman doesn't defend himself anymore. He just adds, rather wearily, that it was he who had wanted it all the time; up until they went to the minister last Saturday, she was set against it and wouldn't go.

Manuel becomes absolutely sober.

"I didn't think you were *so* stupid," he says. "You couldn't really be *so* stupid, could you?"

Åman's eyes wander in anguish from one to the other and clearly tell them that he has already given the answer himself—

"Thanks a lot, Åman!"

By that Borggren means this time that there's got to be a limit to what a person can babble about.

Then Albert finds that Borggren is probably a little bit conceited, and for a change he pokes at that conceit.

"Say, how about that fiancée you had. . . ."

A vein swells across the bridge of Borggren's nose and he clenches one fist. But he is able to control himself.

"She died," he says and swallows with forced calm.

It is a painful scar although it is eight years old; it hurts to this day.

Divertingly he says:

"That goddamn preacher over in the mission chapel . . . ."

Manuel comes to his assistance:

"Yes, that guy. I'll bet he's a phony. . . ."

ONCE MORE THEY HEAR ÅMAN BRING UP HIS PERSON.
Or rather his father.

"I can't remember much of him; he too died so early. Then mamma remarried and I was left with relatives until I'd finished school. Then mamma died. My stepfather had a farm, it was said; that's where I was to go. But when I got there, the farm had been taken to clear the debts, so I had to work as a farmhand. And a farmhand I've stayed ever since. . . ."

He falls silent for a while. Then he says what he did at the beginning of the party:

"Just imagine that I got to be thirty-five after all."

He can see from the four faces how terribly uninteresting his story is. He pours out the last shots of liquor for them, and in a last effort they become polite, wearily polite.

"Well, thanks a lot, Åman."

"Yes, dammit, thanks, Åman."

He replies that there's still a drop left—

"Yes. No. Take it yourself, Åman."

In solitude he takes out the prediction by the Dutch beard again. The lines run together just a little but that doesn't make them look any more true. And certainly he'll write again, he decides, but for the time being he tears these pages in two, then in two once more, and once more.

He takes off his shoes and puts on the shiny galoshes. Lies down on the sofa and peers straight down into their shine.

THE OLD HIGHWAY

"To court, you say? Not for that silly goose of mine anyway. She won't tell who it is. 'I don't know,' she says. 'You don't know?' I said, and once I got plumb beside myself. I grabbed hold of a hunk of her hair and that hasn't happened this side of her confirmation. 'You don't know!' I said. After all, she hasn't been gallivanting about that much. 'You've surely got some sense in your head,' I said. 'Now out with it! I won't wallop you,' I said. 'Not now, it might be dangerous. But you'll never have another happy day,' I said. 'If you don't tell me where you've been,' I said. 'I won't tell, I'll never tell. Never as long as I live.' She's scared, poor little ninny! And if it's the one I think, then by golly I'm scared too. If it's him, we might as well forget about it; we'll find some way out. And if we leave him alone, maybe he'll fork over a few crowns anyway. But just imagine taking up with a fellow like that! Though of course I know myself, a person is blind for a while at that time. When it gets going. Stone-blind. And you don't believe there'll be one on the way so fast. . . ."

". . . quiet. Let people chitter-chatter. But I keep as quiet as can be. That's best."

"Look there at the organblower! He's going home now to a dinner that isn't even started yet. And no coffee besides. And maybe he has no appetite for either one; it's mostly bicarbonate he refreshes himself with. On account of that everlastingly sour stomach. And then he suffers from insomnia, he says. Lies there tossing and sweating all night."

Now the maid is sick, the farmhand was kicked by the horse, and a cow simply lay down and died.
"It seems like just nothing is going for you now, Per."
"Oh, yes, the clock's going. But it's damned slow."

"Here is the address for you. B. Nilsson, P.O. Box 2097, Stockholm, gives advice about prematurely greying hair."

Elis is bustling about on the highway again; it's about some music sheets. The boy can read the notes, he says. But there's an introduction and that's in German.
"We never thought of that when we wrote for it."
He isn't going to stop; he has farther to go.
"They say there's a damned German living somewhere in the upper parish now."
He's on his way there. But then he stops all the same.
"Look here," he says and begins to leaf through the sheets. "This is what the boy wants to have translated. He thinks it's something about the bow."
Nervous and eager, he has twisted them into such a tight roll that, time after time, the pages slip out of his hands and curl up in each other. The German gets the blame:
"The only time you need those goddamn Germans. They might live a bit closer."
As a matter of fact he's getting less and less sure whether he ought to go on. Whether he's going to find out much more even if he does go on.
"Because supposing the German doesn't know any Swedish?"
He's had so many things go wrong here that another disappointment seems more than likely—he wants neither

to go on nor to turn back; mostly he wants to stay here and talk about what was the real meaning behind the boy's purchase of the double bass.

Wants to say that with it the twenty-year-old musician in a way has got a new lease on life—

"They're remarkable tones. . . ."

But fear is still in his eyes, and hesitancy. He holds out the rolled-up music sheets as a sort of powerless iron rod, as a completely impotent crowbar—he'll have to work the stony field all alone now; the boy can't grip the double bass either with his paralyzed legs.

"And now she's been ruined. Maybe I never thought it would be any different. But thought or no thought, I may say that I've hoped against hope. That things would improve at least some day. That she'd be something like other people. The others, they don't go off the deep end. And if they do, they get away with it. They sure take more bites of the forbidden fruit than anyone knows about."

"Leviathan the piercing serpent, even leviathan that crooked serpent. Isaiah XXVII."

"I believe I've done enough with these alder bushes. I'm just getting sweaty. And I've heard that working till you're sweaty is the most dangerous thing you can do."

"She's never happy these days. And this week she's been sick. It hurts to see her that way. One never gets used to it, never gets hardened. Or calloused, like my mother would say. And then she's heavy already, as you've seen, and she'll stay that way the whole summer. It's been the same with all three of them, that they swell fast and get to looking gawky all at once."

He never got as far as the German. He turned back home and said to hell with the bow; it sounds quite good enough as it is.

And then a letter has come which he thinks showed he was right about the canceled walk up to the German.

"Because they have a band down there."

The boy had written to ask if he could take his double bass with him. And, as he said, got a real nice letter back.

And now he's leaving—

Because they didn't state in the letter that he should *not* leave. Although he's perfectly well, except for his legs.

Elis repeats the dead-certain but incredible fact:

"So now he'll be leaving soon."

And helplessly, to the obstruction of nothing:

"That is, if we manage to get him down to the bus, of course."

But, oh! they'll manage! that's not a heavy load any longer, counted quite simply in kilos.

"Just half a boy's body. So to speak. . . ."

"I keep looking at people. Like those who go into the forest and labor and toil. And eat. And are so serious they don't see that there's something comical about themselves.

"They won't believe that they have any joy inside."

"So they aren't moving?"

"No, they aren't. And of course he exaggerated. It wasn't a particularly wild party; I've seen a lot worse. We just kept on till two, maybe three. But hardly anyone was singing. And why didn't he come down and join the party? Instead of pacing back and forth up there all by himself? They say he came down at eight. And woke them up and told them that now they had to move on the first.

'I can't stay up like that anymore,' he said. And then Sunday went by. Until he got that message in the afternoon that his twin brother had jumped out of his attic window in the city. And had been taken to the hospital and was almost dead. He came back late at night. And woke them up again. And said, 'Let's forget about it. Let's forget about what happened earlier. I was so nervous and cranky,' he said. 'But now I'm quite calm and cool. He will die soon and you don't have to move; I was just so nervous last night. I'm going to bicycle back to him now. I'm quite calm and cool....' "

"I've decided to lie flat on my back. Because if I die now, I'll save them from having to straighten me out for the funeral."

"That's some crazy jaunt she went on. He's certainly not right in the head; I can tell by his forehead. That there's something missing. She never has talked about him. 'Is it him?' like I said at the outset, but it was totally impossible to get an answer out of her. Just scared stiff, like I said. And she doesn't care for him. And that's probably a real blessing when all's said and done. At least I'm happy about it."

So just one more evening left; he states briefly what it will involve.

"We are going to pack."

He's carrying quite a little load of wrapping paper that he got from Blomkvist in the store; they'll need some great big sheets for the double bass. They haven't bought a bag for it yet, and now there's no time. He'll have to get himself one when he reaches Göteborg.

Get himself one, yes; everything possible shall be gotten. Night clothes, for example, they wrote about night clothes. There's something *called* night clothes—

Then he says:

"But suppose this is the only trip he'll ever take? You want to send him off as well as you can."

A smile comes to his lips; he's thinking about how there are always resources to draw on when it really matters.

"I haven't quite figured it out yet. . . ."

He adds it all up again in his head. Then puts his fist over his chin and mouth, over that inappropriate satisfaction which he feels is there. But which is not in his mind, in his heart.

"I'll be damned," he says more firmly. "It won't stop at three hundred crowns. A new suit, a new coat. And a new suitcase."

"You can't teach others anything. Everybody has to learn for himself. You can only help others."

"Yes, that's right, she's been to see the minister. He sent for her. 'Look, this is just so stupid,' he said. 'That you won't talk about it. That you won't tell the child's paternity,' he said. And 'Yes!' that almighty silly goose says. 'It is stupid. I won't be so stupid next time.' You can imagine how horrified he got, that minister boy. 'Next time!' he said. 'There mustn't be any next time, don't you understand!' And she turned crimson red, she told me when she came back home. So red it burned, she said. 'No, that wasn't what I meant,' she said that she had said. And that she'd got redder and redder. And he turned red, she said. 'I felt so sorry for him; he's just a boy,' she said. Nice. I've heard several people say that, anyway. Say that he's thought to be a good sort."

Astrid Blomkvist poured a bag of beans into a pea box by mistake. Now she's sorting them out.

"It's like in the fairytales. About the princess who had

to sort out the beans in such and such a short time. To satisfy the evil queen."

"I'm not sure. Perhaps it'll fade. It probably will."
"Well, sure, Blomkvist. We all fade, don't we. And that's the way it goes."
She wants the dress material anyway, mostly out of bitterness. Out of spite.
"That skinflint. He won't fork out one cent. And here I have to...."
Then she pushes the price tag back again; she wants to buy a toy first. A car.
"He didn't get one for Christmas."
Two are small and inexpensive, only one crown and twenty-five öre, according to Blomkvist's pencil scratchings. But he himself thinks that's high.
"For six or seven nails. And about as much wood as in a cigar box."
"I may take the cheapest material," she answers him. "But the car must be just right. This one?"
"That'll run you three crowns. And this five. Imagine, a full five crowns!"
He does not approve of her extravagance. She's peevish, he can hear. That she's got the kid peevish—that he knows.
"They just point at something and they get it. It wasn't like that when I was a kid. I don't recall having any other toys than a rusty old knife that I fiddled around and slashed myself with."

"No, she doesn't cry; none of them cried. She just stays quiet. I bought shoes for her yesterday; Blomkvist had got in some with a strap. 'Are her feet really that small?' he said."

"They were wicked. And above all stingy. They bought a farm. And after a while someone asked the old farm-hand what he thought of his new bosses. 'I'll not say anything about the master and mistress,' he said. 'But the earth, the goddamn earth that has to carry such skunks!' "

"If a person had known as much when he was twenty as he knows now. I was well over thirty before I caught on to things."

He holds Beda up to ridicule again:

"I guess we'd been married some eight or ten years. And then I remember one evening I'd gone to bed and Beda was still puttering around. She was doing the dishes. 'Leave that till tomorrow,' I said. 'You come on to bed too.' 'I'll be there directly,' she said. 'I just want to finish the dishes.'

"So a good while went by.

" 'Come on now,' I said.

"Same reply.

"And finally I thought:

" 'Oh hell, you can just stay there, too!'

"It was around midsummer as I recall. Yes, it was the day before midsummer's eve. A stylish American girl dressed in yellow was sauntering around here. But she's too chancy for me, I thought. Instead I made a date with one of the maids. But as I was going home later on, who do you think I ran into? And that was at three in the morning, maybe at four. Yup, you guessed it, the yellow American girl. That's how utterly stupid you can be. Just plain stupid. Until it's too late. The only consolation you have is that women aren't always so smart themselves either. Not like they think they are, anyway; Beda wasn't, that's for sure. And she has suffered plenty for it, believe me. In a way I feel sorry for Beda, I sometimes do."

"Two öre more a liter, is that too much? Don't you think I deserve it? For having to pull at those crappy cows."

"I wonder if we're going to get a rainshower? Things sure do need it now. Well, so long."

"If I live to be a hundred, I won't forget it. How they came along the road and up this hill. And now I'll tell you what I've never told a single soul before. I can't get it into my sinful skull that they were here on the Lord's business. They didn't look like it. Not because they were in black, that was all right seeing that Helga was so sick. And maybe I shouldn't have pushed them away like I did. Shouldn't have said that she was so terribly ill. Maybe I should have made things out to be a little better than they were so they wouldn't have become so eager. There was an evil glint in Samuel's eyes. 'You weren't really planning to stand in our way?' he said. 'I have witnesses here; nothing will be done that is not in full justice. But you mustn't try to stop us in this mission; it's a dangerous thing to stand in the way of Jesus.' I guess she heard this in there where she was lying; there's such an echo in the glass porch. If she didn't hear the words, then at any rate she heard the tone of voice. And then she wanted to save me from trouble, I think, as sick as she was. 'You may come in now,' we heard her say. 'Because later on I want to be quite alone.' So in they strode. And then I did another stupid thing. I thought everything would keep on as peacefully as it began; none of them mentioned a will. But I ought to have stayed. At least I ought to have listened at the door. Now they were singing a verse from a song that she liked, quietly and beautifully. Fairly beautifully anyway, and then they read from the Psalms and then they prayed. And so I decided they deserved to be treated as well as possible after that. I sneaked out into the kitchen and prepared some better things than I had before, feeling sorry that I had made things ready for them with a hard and hateful heart—They had got her savings-bank book when I came back in! And a power of attorney! And got her angry with me. 'The house is left to you anyway!' she said. 'And the sewing machine. And there'll be nothing else but hard work; you'll never believe it. . . .' "

"Those little hands of hers. Like little leaves. . . ."

"Can you lend me an umbrella with a long handle? If you have one. I'm going in to the hospital to visit him. Because he took the cane with the silver crook when he left."

"I think things'll go okay for her. I always thought so, like I said. She's not flighty, you'll have to admit. She won't have to be cut off from a steady bed because of this. And now she's stuck for a while and has that to think about. And about the baby when it comes. It all takes time. And then she'll be older."

"She's so fat and potbellied. And waggling and wobbling with her behind so I didn't recognize her at all."

"Hello. How are things?"
"Just fine, thanks."
"And how is your mother?"
"Oh. She's dead and gone."

"I haven't been out much this summer. See? You can hardly tell from the grass that I've been walking there. Only a little ripple in it, kind of, from my footsteps."

"When I was weaving these curtains, I got tired, so tired. My eyesight is so bad nowadays. I got up in the morning and wove from four to six. Before I went out to the animals. And at night I kept going till twelve and one. But then I got bad pains in my head; well, not really inside, they were on the outside. It was as if a big, strong man was pulling my hair, it was as if each hair had been pounded into my skull with a hammer and nails. As soon as I'd woven for a while, that man came and pulled and pulled my hair. Finally I thought I'd go crazy all over. But the curtains were real nice."

With a face as drawn and pale as a parsnip.

"Maybe he lies awake sometimes at night. And cries because he has no mother. That's what I've imagined myself. . . ."

" 'Say, this is good coffee,' I said. 'It's not the new rye is it?' Stingy female! She put in three coffee beans, at the most, I'll bet. And if she turned the handle of the grinder once around, that'd be the utmost, too."

"Now the sun is setting. So one more day goes from our time. And never comes again, oh yes. That's a good thing! Because it's been a hell of a day!"

"She won't be buried this Sunday. It's not convenient then. In the meantime she will be embalmed. And in at the undertaker's, they thought she'd keep."

Her only child comes home from school with a new geography book and a new atlas.
"It's going to be fun learning this," she says. "Spain. And Asia. . . ."

"And so Old Folks' Day turned out to be at the last possible moment this year too. They had nothing but bunches of rowanberries in the containers on the radiators. And three marigolds in a glass on the pulpit."

"A time to embrace, and a time to refrain from embracing."
Says Ecclesiastes.

"This morning when I woke up I was feeling low, I'll tell you. Real low. I've never felt so low."
"It's no fun, that's for sure. It's much worse than being furious. Because when you're furious, you feel good too. In a way."

First he runs his thumb over a tissue paper with handkerchiefs underneath. Then he considers a white shirt, then again the handkerchiefs. At last he buys a snuff box and the shirt. He describes how he trimmed the Christmas tree, hung all the candy sticks on one side since Alfred probably will have to stay in bed now. And won't be able to get up and look at the other side.

"I'm sick and tired of loaning my silk dress to her. Every time she goes to a party. She sweats so badly under the arms and just ruins it for me. So now I've taken it in at the seams. From now on she'll have to use a shoe horn if she wants to squeeze into it!"

"... like those totem poles in Alaska; they are God. Greasy and repulsive and full of the most hideous animals. But they are God."

"Maybe you don't believe in God either? You should have bought my Christmas magazine instead of that muck; that would have shown you. 'If I have God's displeasure,' it said, 'then I'm more miserable than a newborn calf. But when He nods his approval to me, then I am nobler than the whole world. When I am allowed to run with the gentle rein which the merciful God uses . . . ."

"Yes, maybe one should read more than one does. When I lived west in Mölnerud, I started to read through the Bible from the beginning to find out exactly what was in it. I got quite far, all the way to Judges. But when I upped and took over the store here, then I never got the time anymore."

"You should subscribe to *The Sower*, Enok. This year. It raises questions there that really make you think. Like about man who shall eat his bread by the sweat of his brow. 'But have you considered,' it said, 'that there are many who are willing to sweat but who can't get work? Does that mean that Punishment is at an end? Or are we to expect something still more terrible? And you who are asking,' it said, 'have you thought of all those who earn their bread and more without shedding a single drop of sweat?' And Moses! He was just a man who was ahead of his times; he didn't perform any miracles. There was a professor who wrote about it. The Red Sea was a natural phenomenon, and he himself had picked manna in the desert. And the water which gushed forth had been there all the time. Just behind a very thin layer of rock."

"I'm sure you're right; I can feel it when I chew with these long teeth that I got for Christmas. 'There's a shortage of teeth now,' the technician said, 'so they may not be a perfect fit. They may be a little longer than they really should be for you,' he said. I'll say they're longer than they should be."

"Hello there. What are you up to?"

"I'm cutting charcoal wood these days. But I haven't started yet."

Lena is there with the usual milk bottle. And Kerstin with a letter about cement. For them, she tells that Gösta is freezing at Boden, where the army is stationed. She has a heart for others besides, for the Russians who are so wretchedly cold that they run right into the tents of the Finns to get warm.

Arne is sending off a calf carcass by bus today. "We're getting too little milk," he says. "And supposing the poor thing starved? Or supposing he was sickly. I've never seen a calf like that. Bristly instead of having hair. Almost like a hedgehog."

"Say, Persson. Did you sweep the bus when you got home last night?"

"No, not last night. But I swept it this morning. About an hour ago."

"And you didn't find a gold ring?"

She's not out of breath, not worried; there was a merry swing in her skirt when she came and it's still there.

"Did you sweep thoroughly?"

Yes, Persson considers that he did.

"On Monday mornings especially I sweep most thoroughly."

"Yes, and next Monday," she answers to this, "next Monday Gösta will be coming home from Boden."

But she is not flustered about the ring as she would have been about some real misfortune or shame.

"I had it in my purse. Like this. And I distinctly thought I saw it when I took out my handkerchief in there. You remember where I was sitting. . . ."

She gazes into the bus, but not so much at the floor as at the people who are in there. And more candidly than they look at her.

There's a holiday again in the middle of this week. And so she asks Persson if he's going to drive then, too, to

the dance. Somehow she's ready to go right now; she has
her purse; she has on her patent leather shoes and her
Sunday blouse, the same one as yesterday.

Persson pulls at the gear shift, and she waves. Remembers the ring again.

"Please sweep once more," she calls. "Tonight. Maybe
it's still lying in a crack somewhere."

"Saying peace, peace, when there is no peace." Jere-
miah.

Kerstin has the baby in her arms.

"Tomorrow I'm taking him to the doctor. See how
awful he looks!"

He's got scurvy.

"Don't you think he looks awful?"

But Lena thinks he's just fine, in spite of the scurvy.
She waits until Tyra has swung off a good distance on her
walk back. Then she says:

"Why don't you bring the baby with you and. . . ."

Says it in a low voice and then immediately falls silent.

"It's not so lightly said. . . ."

And not until when they are about to part:

"What if I go along with you to the doctor? I don't understand this. I felt so sure I would become pregnant this
spring at last. The way Arne and I have been slaving and
trying so hard. That I should be such a good-for-nothing
. . . ."

She doesn't look at Kerstin, not at the baby either—she
fixes her eyes stubbornly in the direction of the forest, toward the wisps of mist behind it.

"Why don't you bring the boy? And come visit us some
evening. And spend the whole evening. Maybe Arne and
I could get one too, at last. I think you are a bringer of
blessedness. . . ."

"It's all right as long as the heart doesn't jump up so high that you have to *bite* it."

"I'm scared. Last night I was real scared."
"It'll be nice when we get phone service at night. Then I'll stay up till the wee small hours one night. And I'll call Johan. 'Are you still awake too?' I'll say. 'Aren't you asleep?'"

"All things are full of labor, man cannot utter it." Ecclesiastes I:8.

"She suffers from inner disharmony. And nothing is ever good enough for her."

"Well, there was an accursed streak of Satan himself in that woman, besides."

"Exactly where is your brother buried? I know it's near the mortuary. But is it farther up?"
"Yes, farther up."
He has already turned away and says it over his shoulder.
"And to the left? Where the ivy is?"
Now he stops; there's no escape now.
"No. There's nothing on it."
She knew that, or she had thought it might be so. But above all she knows that the loneliness won't be any easier no matter which shoulder he spars with.
"I wanted to go there with a geranium some day. And plant it there."
"Thank you."
There's been no sign of him during the whole winter.
"For that matter, you could come and get the geranium yourself, I imagine."

"Yeah, I could do that."

She draws on his brother for help. Prods with him.

"He will surely think it was nice."

Now he is standing with them as if it were yesterday. And not sometime last fall.

"Just think," she says, "how big and fat he was. And how strong. . . ."

But then the withered survivor of the two suddenly comes to life, extends his mittened hands—

"And how changed he became!"

He means right after death. And strokes his face with the mitten.

"It's better when they're wasted away. They look more ready then."

"Her face appeared to me, and vanished from me. It appeared like beauty itself, and then appeared not, because this beauty was unspeakable; for in her face there was the radiance of a flaming light, such as the light is to the angels in the third heaven, and this made my sight dim, so that I was struck with amazement."

A WINTER DAY

SHE HAS SHOVELED SNOW ALL MORNING LONG. BUT IT LOOKS like it was mostly in vain—the path to the cowshed is already blocked with new drifts; the north wind swirls right across it. It doesn't look too good from the porch steps to the gatepost either—not if she compares with Per at Torphaget; he has made almost a kind of avenue through the drifts and now is just smoothing off the walls on each side of it.

Besides, maybe there'll be no funeral. His brother is reported to be better today. She felt a sudden disappointment as she began to prod at the snow here this morning.

More and more of a disappointment the wearier she grew—

"He's eating today," Per had said.

And added that it was a good sign.

She asks before she goes in:

"Eating, you say? What did you manage to get down him?"

But Per has become cocky because of the unexpected improvement; cross as usual, and tight-lipped, he gives himself time to slap the wall smooth with his shovel.

Then he replies that it was an egg.

"Half an egg yolk."

"Thank God," she says.

The same as she said when they came out. She herself can hear that she doesn't sound any more cordial.

Later, while she is preparing her own food, she reflects that an egg yolk, half an egg yolk, does not necessarily betoken a satisfactory appetite.

No, she started off on the wrong foot this morning! And the day just helps to make everything worse; here, now, Skogman from the Old People's Home is stepping across her threshold to tell her that at long last he has killed the cat, one of the cats. And true enough she'd asked him to do it so she'd be spared the everlasting uproar when the wretches flew at each other like tigers with a jumble of rag rugs all around them. But now she is in no mood to feel pleased about the peace of the night ahead—when the killed one will no longer be standing outside yowling while the other one sits in here hissing and spitting, the one that, in lone majesty, is just now yawning and lazily treading down a hollow for himself in the comforter.

"Yes, now you can be in your element," she says. "Now that your father's gone to the *Galatians!*"

And then she *hates* Skogman for a while as he slouches at the table, slurping up the gruel and the coffee that is the murderer's reward—hates him because of the picture that was never taken; as late as yesterday she had sent word to Ragnar Palm to take a picture of Fredrick before the end.

Now she'll have to cancel it.

Skogman burps.

"Don't you sulk," he says. "Why, Lovisa's in the hospital. . . ."

That's news.

"And this is how it happened," says Skogman. "She was going from her room in the wing to get fresh milk for that miserable cat she'd dragged along with her when she moved in here. The cat she's fattened and fattened so that skunk looks like an oblong soccer ball now. Then she slipped on the cement step where some of the morning milk had probably slopped over and frozen to ice. And broke her thigh bone.

"So like I said, don't sulk. I can take the other deuce of a cat too if you want. And I'll tell you I'm going to miss Lovisa."

Reverently he clasps his hands over his full stomach and burps again.

"Now all I have is you. . . ."

She isn't sulking anymore; the tension around her scalp has let up both because of the news and because of Skogman's mood.

"I think I'll set some dough today," she says. "Then you can come here tomorrow and have a loaf."

THE GARLAND IN BLOMKVIST'S STORE IS PALE, AND THE PLY-wood angel is just plain blue with cold—Ada Karlsson stands there boasting about how well her *red* potatoes have held out. They have cellar space together; Ada has the left bin, and she herself has the one on the right. There are four Karlssons to feed, sometimes five. Who would believe it, that there are so many of the red ones left and the yellow ones have sunk down so fast.

But only the living cat, and he alone, shall hear the slightest hint about this when she gets back with her purchases.

"I'll tell you, Daniel, this cellar rent is getting expensive!"

To Emma Loback, who comes to sit and have coffee, she says nothing about the potatoes and nothing about the green wood that Karlsson carted over. She takes her along out to the henhouse while the coffee is brewing.

"Did you ever see such gleaming white china nest-eggs, now tell me?"

She smiles at Emma's blank face.

"They were gone for two days. But yesterday there they were again. All clean and white. Had been boiled with the others."

They walk back to the kitchen in high spirits.

But she still has to be on her toes a bit even with Emma Loback; she got help from her last fall when she was sick. Help and song, song from morning till evening. And if she can't find something to talk about now, Emma is sure to begin to warble again—that's why she puts the album down by her. She has moved the album and some other trinkets out of the best room over the holidays. It's so cold in there, but it's the same with the sticks of dry wood as with the potatoes; they've been used up quickly. Now she dares have a fire only in the kitchen. The confectioner was named Daniel once upon a time. And in company, like now with Emma Loback, she can see clearly what a funny love story this was; she laughs at the old picture, laughs scornfully at that much too fair-skinned face, that face *with no eyebrows at all!*

"Ha ha!" She pushes away the thought of him as by far the most ridiculous of all her thoughts.

"I remember that he gave me a seed; I never got around to planting it. I left it lying on the mantlepiece for a long time. How he carried on and on about that seed! Later I planted it. But it was nothing more than an ordinary aspidistra."

Yet his orange twig has grown to be a big tree which reaches from floor to ceiling in her best room—fortunately orange trees don't need too much heat, but she does set a big pan of hot water beside it at night.

And in her loneliness—it'll be fifteen years this New Year's Eve—she can almost grab hold of his silly blond hair, can accuse him in the silence, and ask forlornly and at the same time with lips compressed:

"Why did you have so darned—so darned little guts?"

SHE STRUGGLES ALONG WITH HOT WATER FOR THE TWO COWS too—she is aware that the people in the cottages around are snickering, but *her cows truly can't drink it cold.*

Chilled to the bone by the wind, with snow under her skirts, snow in her wooden shoes, she gathers courage and living warmth for the night from Rosa and Bella.

That's her most pressing errand.

Her nephew in Göteborg has written her that she ought to get herself a telephone. But when the daylight comes again, she'll think, as she always has before, that it's too expensive. She has a pair of galoshes from him, and she sets those out so evildoers can see that there's a man in the house. Next summer, if by chance he should make his way over here again at long last, she's going to ask him if he doesn't have a pair of old topboots too; that would be cheaper than a telephone.

And perhaps as serviceable.

Her bed on the kitchen sofa is as narrow as a coffin. But she fits into it; she lies on her back with her hands sedately clasped over her breast.

And two small, grey braids rest just as quietly on the pillow.

And now she has worried enough for today; now she has barred things up all around her—with a hasp and crosspin at the outer door, with a bolt, and with the key turned twice in the lock.

Besides, there are four chairs standing in a row for them to trip over, the evil ones, before they get any farther into the room. And the kitchen balance lies in readiness on the sink; she is going to hit back as long as she has the strength.

> Judas' kiss and Peter's oaths,
>   Caiaphas' and Annas' frauds,
>   And Pilate's soul with fearsome flaws,
> Along with Herod's prideful boasts,
> Show us well, no one dare try
> Upon this world to rely.

The hymnbook, the old one, is still lying on the chest-of-drawers. But in the dark she unclasps her hands anyway and follows the lines with her forefinger and her inner eye.

IT'S NO VILLAIN; IT'S PER AT TORPHAGET WHO IS KNOCKING.
"August is real sick again, real sick," he says. "You'd better come over and see. If he's as sick as I think."
Startled, dazed with sleep, she answers dully:
"Thank God. Yes, he's probably very sick, you know."

Per has been knocking at other doors; three old men from the neighborhood stand bewilderedly rubbing their backs against the wallpaper.
And of course August at Torphaget is on the way out; anyone can see that. His death won't be much of a loss; it was always a poor life of a man who just knocked around and got messed up in liquor during the years when he might have done something useful.

She alone comes to think that, all the same, he did deserve a doctor, he just like anyone else. She trots off to the parish room and makes a phone call, stops by her own place and gets the cactus which bloomed at Christmas as well as a better penholder than the one Per has. The old county medical examiner just writes and writes as long as there's a breath left in a poor soul. He finds it easier to charge the fee then.

She herself might as well dress up now as later, the black silk dress and a spanking white apron.

And so it is a new day. August is gone; the doctor came half an hour after it happened and sat and fidgeted as usual before he managed to say that he wanted twenty crowns.

A white paper is lying on the table.

The old men have trooped out.

Now she's reading Per the text for Epiphany. When the funeral will be.

A SUMMER PLAY

OH, THEY'RE JUST LIKE A PICTURE POSTCARD, A POSTER, A short story as they walk along the road the second day! Imagine Agnes at Kyrkåsen—yes, so little and trim, just as she always was, and as dainty as a doll!

As a matter of fact, we didn't remember that she was so shapely.

And he is a Goliath, a giant in stature; he has arms that could go clear around her—this is what she found in America, the youngest girl at Kyrkåsen. She could fit into one of his big hands; she could jump up and sit there, and he could carry her with him!

Just like a picture postcard, a poster, a short story.

An American fairytale about a troll and a princess.

But then, of course, David enters the scene. He has met them and said hello and chatted and walked along with them a little way. He's a fickle little fellow, this David; he's a bachelor and rich and has a brother in America. Talks easily with people and describes things easily. Now he stares off toward the bend beyond the bridge where they disappeared. He tells what the giant's face looks like, says that he has an eagle nose and dove eyes.

An eagle with dove eyes.

As for the dove, Agnes at Kyrkåsen, Mrs. Goliath, that is—but David is no teller of fairytales; instead, right in the middle of the May day and the sound of rushing stream, he punches a hole through the picture postcard, through the poster:

"By golly, she's been getting it plenty."

Believes in neither dove nor princess, plucks the dove's feathers.

"It's a fact," he says. *"That's* what the women at Kyrkå-sen have always wanted."

Oh no, no fairytale.

"Descended from whoring stock, as you know."

Bachelor, rich, loose-tongued.

"Did you notice the way she walks?"

Old Agnes at Kyrkåsen all over.

AND OF COURSE THERE MAY BE SOME TRUTH IN THAT. BUT IN any case the giant—Algot is his name—seems to be a good-natured man in his manner as well as in his speech—what little we can understand of the latter since he has trouble with the language. Now people go around repeating his comment that he's never felt so good anywhere as here on the porch seat, imitate how he struggles to translate into Swedish what's so good about it.

"*Sailens,*" it sounds like he says first. "Oh, *sailens....*"

It's so silent here, he wants to say.

Evald at the parish house has bought a car; that makes three in just one small place like this. It couldn't possibly be any worse in America.

"Ha!" says Goliath. "*Sri? Sri kars?* Three?"

He opens his mouth wide and laughs.

Agnes is there and translates, and she laughs too, but in her mouth it sounds a little condescending.

It doesn't sound that way in the mouth of the giant.

They talk about acres, that Kyrkåsen is six acres. Algot says he thinks it's better with six than with six hundred.

More about cars on the next day.

About the minister who said that in America they have signboards at dangerous curves and crossroads with a skull and crossbones on them. And about Anders at Bäcka who then replied that in our town now they drive about so madly that it wouldn't do any good if they hung up the whole skeleton.

Agnes laughs.

Algot laughs when he catches on, but still more gently than she.

DAVID IS THERE EVERY DAY ON THE PORCH SEAT. HE HAS THE time and the reasons and the cash; he can work if he wants to and quit if he wants to.

Algot knows David's brother. *Did* know him, he goes on to explain. Better than he does now he wants to say. And for a while it is clear that he is wondering and searching his mind for an explanation of why they don't know him so well now.

They are talking about other things.

But suddenly Algot returns to that brother of David's in America, says he wishes he could have brought fresh greetings for David.

And then he won't let go of the subject.

". . . why did we drift apart? I can't remember. We got on all right together. . . ."

He becomes a little angry, and he brusquely turns to Agnes for help. He wants to know right now why they haven't been seeing as much of David's brother of late. He puts the blame on her and says:

"It was you who got tired. Wasn't that it? Somehow didn't you get tired?"

Now David glosses it over and says that his brother is probably still in Chicago and that he likes it there and that he has no plans for returning home, not very soon anyway.

"We'll look him up," says Algot. "As soon as we get back we'll look him up. In the fall?"

"I guess I should have gone over too," responds David to this. "But it's getting to be too late now. . . ."

He can see that Agnes doesn't help Algot much, neither with the translation nor with the problem about the brother in America. What's more, he can see that he himself is getting help; she waves at him with her shoe and flips her skirt up around her knee.

"You should," she says. "Come on over with us."

She flips up her skirt a good deal more.

"You know, that's the way to live," she continues. "To go abroad."

And, of course, Algot gives her a little help; now he too finally starts boasting about America, even if he isn't quite as enthusiastic as they usually are. And he interrupts himself in his bits of praise and says that it isn't so bad here either.

"Not so bad. . . ."

David treats them to a trip by car; he hires Evald at the parish house, and they go north about two hundred miles, to Algot's childhood home, his home for six years until an uncle took him over to America.

They stay away one night and one day; then Algot sits again on the porch seat and says that the trip was a disappointment. "There just wasn't anything to see," he says. "It's nicer here."

But both David and Agnes say the opposite; of course maybe the childhood home wasn't anything. Though what had he expected? But it was fun in the car. And it was fun at the hotel.

"Oh yes," Algot admits.

Yet the dove eyes are void of pleasure when he admits it.

"ARE YOU REALLY FREE ALL THE TIME?" WONDERS KARI, Agnes' mother. "Have you absolutely nothing to do?"

And David gets the point all right. But that doesn't make him ashamed. Indeed not. He meets her eyes so sharply that she has to look the other way for a while.

"Well, okay," she says. "But to have them come home just so there'll be trouble. . . ."

He laughs right in her face.

"How many troubles did you start? While you were having your heyday. Eh? Not a single one, from what I've heard. It was—well, of course, I've heard something about how it was pretty close once. But that you managed to squeeze your way out. . . ."

Leisurely he gets up and moves closer to her, sways a little and smiles broadly at the glint of agreement in her eyes—shows impudently with his whole expression that in these matters the daughter has nothing to teach the mother. And that they all know it. Except Algot. For his sake they are willing to drive ahead gently—for that matter it's more fun that way—but drive ahead confidently, since the road is passable; David has reconnoitered the terrain, he says.

"My brother wrote . . ."

And dear God, yes. Kari can well imagine that he'd written—

". . . that if Agnes had known her way around before she went to America, heaven knows she hadn't forgotten over there. . . ."

Furthermore Kari reflects that this Goliath seems to no-

tice less than she thought was possible—Going around in
the big world in a sort of daze—

But what if he were to wake up all of a sudden? What
if he wakes up *here?* Can she be so sure that he won't? Can
any of them be so sure of that?

This is what she wanted to talk to David about—that
she'd been thinking since their trip that maybe it's more
usual for some people to become blind in Chicago where
there are so many things to bewilder you, more usual than
here? God knows, what if somebody stone-blind—

And how does a giant react if he should see red all of a
sudden?

They know a lot of things, both she and David and
Agnes—but do they really know anything about how a
dove would react?

A dove which may be an eagle in its way—

Agnes comes upon them as they are testing each other.
And she is quick:

"Don't you worry, mother. Just leave me alone now.
From now until fall. Then we'll be leaving again."

NOT THAT IT'S MONOTONOUS. ALGOT DOESN'T FIND IT MO-
notonous to sit up straight on a porch seat or inside on
the kitchen sofa when it gets cold again around midsummer.

And David also bides his time.

But, after all, they are young people and why shouldn't
they go on another trip.

David speaks belittlingly indeed about what they can
offer a distant traveler around here. "We could go up into
the forest," he says. "I can't think of anywhere else. To
the log cabin. At least it's a little bit away from the civili-

zation down at the parish house. Sometimes we go there in the winter too," he continues, "now and then on Saturday nights. With a phonograph and liquor. *Talk* about women, physical talk. Because mostly we can't get them to go along with us; everything is so watched-over and straightlaced here."

There would be footprints in the snow if nothing else.

"On the other hand traveling Americans must do pretty much what they like. Over there everything is so almighty big; but we choose something trifling instead. We'll walk along a cowpath; we'll come upon a brook and a tarn and a stile and an old charcoal burning ground. And finally upon a chimney and around it the few remains of an old farm cottage, and there we'll just walk around for a while and pick up and turn over what's left, a hearthstone and a horseshoe and a coffee pot. And the headboard of a bed, Agnes . . ." It's midsummer, as we said before, and David is a good storyteller and seems domesticated enough on the porch seat and adds greatly to Algot's good feelings. ". . . the headboard of a bed, Agnes. Now what sort of everlasting wood could that have been made from!

"And we'll gape at an old wild apple tree where the blossoms have knit themselves tightly, tightly into green fruit over every branch—while the apple trees here at home certainly don't overtax themselves. However much we spray them and prune them."

David can easily keep the ball rolling even if he sits here day in and day out.

MIDSUMMER DAY.

Algot is not sitting on the porch seat; he is lying in bed beaten down and sick from too much aquavit.

David isn't there either; he is staying on his own porch seat.

Together with his memory of last night.

So we got there.

And behaved ourselves. Well, we tried to at any rate. For about an hour or so.

But then of course the nips we had brought along began to take effect, and Algot got stoned remarkably fast. And became venturesome, so venturesome that when he grabbed hold of a thigh or tried to stuff his hand down inside a blouse, the girls cooled off and found it awfully easy to look trustworthily and faithfully into the very eyes that were watching them.

And Algot got more liquor, and they used him for a while to excite themselves—Agnes also pressed herself against him and showed how far they could go, even at this point, beneath the hands. That if white showed below the neckline in front or higher up in another place, it was no more than could safely be offered at this hour.

And then the phonograph whined on and they could twist and turn themselves in time to

I-i-in a forest on Mount I-i-ida

and become narrow-eyed and blushing while hard fingers squeezed them on the breasts.

Agnes did it, and the others did it.

But David was the left-over one, was curiously the contented one. He busied himself at the fire, made coffee, ground up coffee in reserve, set the table, changed the records.

You are fai-i-ir, oh Brogren....

And he said nothing when a body suddenly sprawled down across the set table and the record player. Then he relaxed instead, relaxed all his senses. For at that moment he could see, as he cast a sideways glance at Agnes, that he wouldn't get much peace for the rest of the night.

He secretly poured water into his glass and exchanged a toast with Algot.

He is remembering this now.

And in the sunshine, idle and contented with his thoughts, he stretches his white-sleeved arms out toward what followed.

"WELL, IT SEEMS TO BE GOING ALL RIGHT," PEOPLE ARE saying.

Past the hay time, past the rye time, it goes all right.

But then it isn't going all right in the least anymore; David has become remarkably hectic and restless-eyed. For a whole week he stays away from the porch seat, from the steps below.

And then all of a sudden he is back and hires Evald and the car again, but he is just as agitated, if not worse, when they return.

He drives around alone with Evald to other dance pavilions on Saturday nights, and fills him up with long, whining descriptions of his contempt for Kyrkåsen and its incorrigible womenfolk.

And he stands white-faced, leaning against the railing of our dance pavilion after one o'clock, after two o'clock, when Agnes and Algot have gone home again.

And he takes up with any sleepy beardless farmhand about whom she danced with, how often with the same guy?

And when did she come? And when did she go?

NOT UNTIL THE LEAVES ARE YELLOWING IS EVERYTHING again as it once was.

For a couple weeks it's like that.

Then a little storm breaks over Kyrkåsen; Algot is going to return to America alone. They got too bold one evening in September.

A roaring storm. And Kari is whirled along in it; she doesn't have the strength to deny anything. She stands in the store wringing her hands and moaning and saying that of course she suspected this would happen! But why couldn't they have got on their way first—in her confusion she doesn't notice how foolish she sounds; she just asks, why and why?

And so persistently that at last people just laugh at her.

Then she repents of it. For Agnes is cleverer than she, much cleverer.

On the day of departure there is no question but that they are leaving together.

And Agnes is babbling away as usual, no more than usual, not conscience-smitten or anything like that.

Algot is perhaps more silent, and he doesn't eat much. And he looks a little tired, but that isn't necessarily anything besides the thought of the long trip ahead. What other thoughts he may have aren't apparent at any rate.

He was up late last night packing things into suitcases and into the trunk.

And a good half hour before the bus arrives, he is sitting quietly on the porch seat saying his goodbyes. "Well, I wonder when we'll be around here again."

And Kari is out in the garden cutting the last dahlias; she has protected them with newspapers against the frost for three nights now. They make a rather pretty bunch and she has planned to thrust it into Agnes' hands because she feels that she doesn't dare give it to Algot as she had first intended. But however it happened, Agnes' little paws are full of other things at the moment of farewell, a patent leather purse and the like. So Algot gets it after all.

And he accepts it too.

While he is helping the driver, he lays it on the gate-post.

And then they are off.

And the bouquet gets left behind. The mother-in-law runs after them a few yards with it. Then he thrusts his head out through the window, and now there is hatred in his face again—he waves off the flowers she had saved and shouts English words into the strong wind:

"Damn it! Yes! Damn it. . . ."

PUBLISHED IN
THE NORDIC TRANSLATION
SERIES

FROM DENMARK

H. C. Branner, *Two Minutes of Silence*. Selected short stories, translated by Vera Lindholm Vance, with an introduction by Richard B. Vowles. 1966.

Tom Kristensen, *Havoc. Hærværk,* translated by Carl Malmberg, with an introduction by Børge Gedsø Madsen. 1968.

Jacob Paludan, *Jørgen Stein*. Translated by Carl Malmberg, with an introduction by P. M. Mitchell. 1966.

FROM FINLAND

Hagar Olsson, *The Woodcarver and Death. Träsnidaren och döden,* translated by George C. Schoolfield. 1965.

Toivo Pekkanen, *My Childhood. Lapsuuteni,* translated by Alan Blair, with an introduction by Thomas Warburton. 1966.

F. E. Sillanpää, *People in the Summer Night. Ihmiset suviyössä,* translated by Alan Blair, with an introduction by Thomas Warburton. 1966.

FROM ICELAND

Fire and Ice: Three Icelandic Plays, with introductions by Einar Haugen. Jóhann Sigurjónsson, *The Wish (Galdra-Loftur*), translated by Einar Haugen. Davið Stefánsson, *The Golden Gate (Gullna hliðið),* translated by G. M. Gathorne-Hardy. Agnar Thorðarson, *Atoms and Madams (Kjarnorka og kvenhylli),* translated by Einar Haugen. 1967.

Gunnar Gunnarsson, *The Black Cliffs. Svartfugl,* translated by Cecil Wood, with an introduction by Richard N. Ringler. 1967.

FROM NORWAY

Aksel Sandemose, *The Werewolf. Varulven,* translated by Gustaf Lannestock, with an introduction by Harald S. Næss. 1966.
Tarjei Vesaas, *The Great Cycle. Det store spelet,* translated by Elizabeth Rokkan, with an introduction by Harald S. Næss. 1967.

FROM SWEDEN

Tage Aurell, *Rose of Jericho and Other Stories. Berättelser,* translated by Martin Allwood, with an introduction by Eric O. Johannesson. 1968.
Karin Boye, *Kallocain.* Translated by Gustaf Lannestock, with an introduction by Richard B. Vowles. 1966.
Peder Sjögren, *Bread of Love. Kärlekens bröd,* translated by Richard B. Vowles. 1965.

Other translations to come.